Enid Blyton

The Little White Rabbit

...and other stories

Bounty Books

Published in 2015 by Bounty Books,
a division of Octopus Publishing Group Ltd,
Carmelite House
50 Victoria Embankment,
London EC4Y 0DZ
www.octopusbooks.co.uk

An Hachette UK Company
www.hachette.co.uk
Enid Blyton ® Text copyright © 2011 Chorion Rights Ltd.
Illustrations copyright © 2015 Award Publications Ltd.
Layout copyright © 2015 Octopus Publishing Group Ltd.

Illustrated by Linda Worrall.

ISBN: 978-0-75373-053-9

A CIP catalogue record for this book is available from the
British Library.

Printed and bound by CPI Group (UK) Ltd, Croydon, CR0 4YY

CONTENTS

The Little White Rabbit

Mrs Flop-Ear was a big sandy rabbit who lived in a nice little home in Bracken Bank. She had seven children, all sandy like herself, except for one.

He was snowy-white, and Mrs Flop-Ear was really very proud of him. He looked so beautiful when he was a tiny baby rabbit. But when he grew old enough to scamper about he didn't look beautiful any longer.

"I never in my life knew a rabbit who got himself so dirty!" said his mother. "Never! I send him out as clean as can be, washed from head to bobtail – and in ten minutes' time he comes in as black as soot. What do you do with yourself, Bobbo?"

"Nothing," said Bobbo. "I just found some mud and rolled in it, that's all. It was lovely."

"And now I've got to wash you all over again," said Mrs Flop-Ear, tying a big apron round her furry waist. "Come here! No carrot-cake for tea for you today!"

Well, you might have thought that punishments like that would have taught Bobbo to be careful. But they didn't. The very next day he came home covered in green patches.

"Look at Bobbo!" squealed the other rabbits. "He's all green. Look at Bobbo, Ma!"

"And what have you been doing with yourself now, I'd like to know?" asked his mother.

"Nothing," said Bobbo. "I just saw a man painting a fence, and I played with his paint. It was lovely."

"Come here," said Mrs Flop-Ear. "I'll have to clean you with turpentine this time – and it will smell horrid. And I wouldn't be surprised if Pa doesn't wallop you for making the home smell of green paint!"

Bobbo was cleaned with turpentine. He cried. And he cried again when Pa Flop-Ear walloped him with a bracken stalk. Well, well – everyone thought he would have learned his lesson that time.

Not a bit of it! He came home two days later sneezing and spluttering – and his coat was quite black. In fact, nobody recognised him at first when he scampered back to his neat little home down the burrow.

"What's this! Who is it? Hey, get out!"

cried Mrs Flop-Ear, flapping at Bobbo with her duster. It hit him and a cloud of soot flew out from his fur.

"Don't, Ma. It's me, Bobbo, come home to tea," cried Bobbo. Everyone stared. Goodness gracious, was this black creature really the snowy-white bunny?

"Bobbo! Where on earth have you been?" cried Mrs Flop-Ear. "Up a chimney or something?"

"No, I found a sack and slipped inside. It was full of lovely black powder," said

Bobbo. "I did have a glorious time. But it makes me sneeze."

"He's been inside a bag of soot," said poor Mrs Flop-Ear. "Is there anything worse he can do? Come here, Bobbo. Come outside with me. I'll have to beat the soot out of you with bracken fronds. Come, children, you must all help. We shall never get Bobbo white again unless we bang the soot out of his fur."

Poor Bobbo. What a time he had! His mother and all his brothers and sisters banged him with big bracken fronds, and the soot flew out in clouds. Bobbo yelled and shouted, but nobody would stop.

He had to be got clean, because Granny Flop-Ear was coming to visit them the next day. Whatever would she say to a sooty rabbit?

"And now, Bobbo, if you dare to come home dirty before your granny comes, I simply don't know what I'll do with you," said his mother, when he was white and clean again.

He ran out to play with the others the next day, but presently he saw a big barrel standing by the roadside. What was in it? He hopped up to see. My, it was full of some lovely, sticky, black stuff! Bobbo put in both his paws and began to play with it.

Soon he had to go home. The others called him. He jumped down from the barrel and ran over to them. He wiped his paws on the grass, but oh dear, the black sticky stuff wouldn't come off! So he wiped his paws down his furry body and made great black streaks there!

"You look like a zebra!" said the others. "My word, Ma will be angry with you!"

Mrs Flop-Ear *was* angry with him. She gave one look at Bobbo and groaned. "Tar!" she said. "You've been playing with tar. All right, Bobbo, I give up. If you want to be black, you shall be black!"

She took a bottle of black dye. She tipped it into a bath of hot water and the water turned as black as night. She stirred it up. Bobbo came to look – and in a trice his mother swung him up by his long ears and then plunged him into the hot dye.

"Oh! A hot black bath!" said Bobbo. "Oh, how odd! Are the others going to have one too, Ma? Can I have a red one tomorrow? Oh, what are you doing?"

Mrs Flop-Ear stirred him round and round in the black dye. Then she lifted him out by his ears. He was as black as soot! She squeezed him and squeezed him – and then, oh dear, she went outside on the hill, and she pegged him up by his long ears to dry in the wind!

"Ma! Bobbo is quite black now, even his ears and tail," said the other rabbit children in surprise. "What have you done to him?"

"I've dyed him black," said their mother. "He can't get any blacker now. He can't even look dirty! Your grandmother will be very surprised to see I've a black child

when she comes to tea this afternoon!"

Granny Flop-Ear was very surprised. Bobbo wasn't dry when she arrived, and she saw him swinging by his black ears in the wind, hanging on the clothes-line, yelling loudly.

"Take me down! I won't get dirty again! Take me down! I hate being out on the clothes-line! Take me down!"

But Mrs Flop-Ear wouldn't take him down till he was quite dry. She was so afraid of getting black dye over everything if she took him down when he was still wet. So Bobbo had to swing on the line until it was dark.

"Take me down! The fox will come and eat me! Oh, come and take me down!" he shouted.

So he was taken down at last, a little black rabbit who didn't look like Bobbo at all. "I'll be good now," he told his mother. "I won't get into mischief any more."

"Well, you can't get any blacker than you are!" said his mother. "So you should be all right."

But what do you think little black Bobbo is doing this very minute? He's found a pail of whitewash and he's playing with it! He'll go home daubed and splashed with white all over his nice black coat! What are you to do with a little bunny like that?

The Old
Wooden Horse

Donald had a wooden horse that was very old. He had had Dobbin since he was two, and he was now seven, so you can tell how old the wooden horse was.

He had lost all his bright red paint, and his four wheels were rather loose and wobbly. He still had quite a fine mane, but his tail, alas, was gone! His mother did once cut some lengths of wool and tried to stick them on for a tail for Dobbin, but they wouldn't stick. So he hadn't any tail at all, and Donald was always rather sorry about it.

"It makes Dobbin look strange," he thought. "But he's a dear old horse and I love him. I shall never give him away. It would make him unhappy."

Donald always took Dobbin out once a week into the garden. He was fair to all his toys and tried to play with them in turn, so that none of them should feel left out. He thought it must be dreadful to be put on a shelf and not taken any notice of at all for months and months.

So Dobbin was taken out into the garden and ridden on every Saturday that was fine. Donald could ride on him quite well by scuffling along the ground with his feet. Then Dobbin ran along on his four wheels.

Now one day a most extraordinary thing happened. It was all because Donald thought of taking Dobbin into the lane that ran at the bottom of the garden.

"We'll go out of the gate into the lane and go to the oak-trees there and see if any acorns are falling," said Donald to Dobbin. "It is such a very, very windy day that I expect there will be heaps."

So out of the gate and into the lane they went. Donald rode on Dobbin to the oak-trees – and when he got there he stopped in surprise.

Somebody else was there! It was a small man with a very long beard, a green tunic, and an enormously large

hat with a yellow feather in it! He was collecting acorns in a basket.

He didn't see Donald because he had his back to him. He didn't hear him coming either, because the wind was making such a tremendous noise in the trees.

Donald sat still on Dobbin and watched the little man in surprise. He felt certain that he was looking at a brownie – one of the fairy-folk – because he really was just exactly like the pictures of one.

The little man was humming a strange song in a very deep voice. Then suddenly the wind blew extra hard and tugged at the brownie's hat. The little man put up his hand at once to hold it on – but he was too late. The marvellous hat flew off in the wind, its yellow feather waving wildly.

"Oh! Oh! My beautiful hat! My lovely,

perfectly splendid, beautiful hat!" cried the brownie, and he dropped his basket of acorns on the ground.

The wind took the big hat right away down the lane. The brownie began to run after it, still shouting, "Oh, my hat, my beautiful hat!"

Then he suddenly saw Donald sitting on Dobbin. "Hello!" he cried. "Lend me your horse, will you? I'll never catch my hat unless I ride after it!"

"But Dobbin is only made out of wood!" said Donald. "He can't go by himself!"

"Oh, don't waste time telling me silly things like that!" cried the brownie, and he pushed Donald off his horse. He got on Dobbin himself and smacked the wooden horse on the neck.

"Gee-up!" he yelled. "Gee-up!"

And, my goodness gracious me, Dobbin shook off his wheels, kicked out his legs, and galloped after that enormous hat! You should just have seen him! Donald stood there under the oak-trees, staring after Dobbin and the brownie as if he really couldn't believe his eyes!

"What a very extraordinary thing!"

Donald kept saying to himself. "I can't believe it! I really can't!"

Soon the brownie and Dobbin were out of sight. Donald wondered what to do. He was left there with a basket half full of acorns and four wheels belonging to Dobbin!

He filled the basket with acorns and then picked up the wheels to take them home. He was sure that he would never see Dobbin again.

But he did! In a few minutes there came the sound of galloping, and back came the wooden horse carrying the brownie on his back – and the little man was wearing his enormous hat once more!

"I've got it!" he cried. "Wasn't it a bit of luck? I caught it all right! But I say – a dreadful thing has happened! Poor old Dobbin has lost his tail – now don't cry, don't make a fuss, please. I'll put it right, yes, really I will! He must have lost it in his mad gallop after my hat. I'm more sorry than I can say. But I can put it right – yes, I can. Just watch me. And don't say a word, please, don't worry about it. I promise I can put it right."

Donald couldn't get a word in. The brownie talked so hard and wouldn't stop. Donald wanted to say that Dobbin had lost his tail ages ago, but it wasn't a bit of good. As soon as he opened his mouth the brownie talked more loudly than ever!

He took out a pair of scissors from his tunic pocket. He snipped a big piece off his lovely grey beard. He twisted it until it

made a fine tail. He rubbed some yellow stuff from a little jar on to Dobbin's tail-end, and then slapped the bit of beard on to it – and in a trice it grew there! It really and truly seemed as if it grew. It not only grew there, but it wagged itself. It was perfectly wonderful.

"Oh my!" said Donald, astonished. "I never saw anything like that before, never! Why, little man, Dobbin hasn't had a tail for ages. I kept trying to tell you. Now he has a really beautiful, waggy tail, and I am pleased."

"Are you really?" asked the brownie, delighted. "Then I'm pleased too. Very pleased. It was good of you to let me have

Dobbin to ride after my hat. I'd never have got it back if you and he hadn't just happened to be here. Very lucky thing for me."

Dobbin had set himself back on his wheels as soon as Donald had put them back on the ground. There he stood, a good, quiet, little wooden horse again, looking as if he had never, never galloped in his life!

"Will he ever gallop off again when I'm on him?" asked Donald. "I would so like that."

"I shouldn't be surprised," said the brownie, setting his hat straight and picking up his basket of acorns. "Once a horse has found his feet, he's always likely to use them again. Well – goodbye, and many thanks."

He ran off down the lane, holding his enormous hat safely on his head. The yellow feather waved in the wind. Donald got on to Dobbin's back and clicked to him.

"Gee-up! Gallop with me!"

But Dobbin didn't. Donald was so disappointed. He took Dobbin in to his mother and told her all that had happened. "And if you don't believe me, well, just look at Dobbin's tail!" he said. "It's made out of a bit of the brownie's grey beard, Mum – really it is!"

Dobbin hasn't galloped off yet. I hope I am there when he does!

The Inquisitive Hedgehog

There was once a most inquisitive hedgehog who liked to know everybody else's business. He used to shuffle round the ditches, listening to all that the toad said to the frog, and trying to find out where the squirrel had hidden his winter nuts.

The pixies that lived in the hedgerow were most annoyed with him for he was always trying to find out their secrets, and, as you know, pixies have many magic secrets which no one but themselves must know. Whenever they met together to talk they had to be sure to look under the dead leaves or behind the ivy to see if Prickles the hedgehog was hiding there, ready to listen.

Now one day a wizard called Tonks came to visit the pixie Lightfoot, who lived in a small house in the bank of the hedgerow. This house had a little door hung over with a curtain of green moss, so that no one passing by could see it.

Inside the door was a cosy room with little tables, chairs, and couches, for Lightfoot often had parties and needed plenty of furniture. There was a small fireplace at one end, and on it Lightfoot boiled his kettle and fried his bacon and eggs for breakfast.

Tonks was to come and have a very

important talk with Lightfoot and the other pixies about the party that was to be given in honour of the Fairy Princess's birthday the next winter. Prickles overheard the toad telling the little brown mouse, and he longed to know what day the party was to be, and if the creatures of the hedgerow were to be invited as well as the fairy-folk.

But nobody could tell him, for nobody knew. "Nothing is decided yet," said the toad. "And even when it is, I don't suppose we shall know until the invitations are sent out, Prickles. You must just be patient."

"Yes, but you see, I want to go and visit my grandmother who lives far away on the hillside," said Prickles. "And if I choose the week when the party is held, it would be most unfortunate."

"Well, we shan't miss you very much," said the toad, going under his stone. He was not fond of the inquisitive hedgehog at all.

Prickles wondered and wondered how he could get to know what the pixies would say when Tonks the wizard came to talk with them. And at last he thought of an idea.

"If I creep into Lightfoot's house just before the pixies and the wizard go there to meet, and cover myself with a cloth, I shall look like a sofa or a big stool, and no one will notice me. Then I can lie quietly under my cloth and hear everything!" he thought to himself. "What a good idea!"

So he borrowed a red shawl from the old brownie woman who lived in the hazel copse, and stuffed it into a hole in the bank where an old wasps' nest had once been. Then he waited impatiently for the evening to come when Tonks was to see the hedgerow pixies.

At last it came. Prickles took his shawl out of the hole and went to where the green moss-curtain hung over Lightfoot's little door. As he crouched there, looking like a brown clod of earth, the door opened and Lightfoot ran out. He was going to fetch some cakes. He left his door open, and Prickles quickly went inside. The room was neatly arranged with the chairs and stools in a circle. Prickles pushed them about and made

room for himself. He threw the red shawl over his prickly back and crouched down, looking like a couch without a back, or a great stool! He was pleased. Now he would hear everything!

Very soon Lightfoot came back. He was humming a little tune. He put out the cakes neatly on a dish which he placed on a table, and set the kettle on the fire to boil water for some tea.

Presently there was a knocking at the door. Lightfoot opened it. In came the pixies from the hedgerow, chattering and laughing.

"Find seats for yourselves!" said

Lightfoot. "I'm just making the tea. I've some cakes, too, if you'd like to help yourselves."

"We'll wait till old wizard Tonks comes!" said the pixies. They sat down on the chairs and began to talk. Prickles listened hard with both his ears, hoping to hear a few secrets.

Rat-tat-tat! Someone knocked loudly on the door. It was Tonks the wizard. Lightfoot ran to open it, and bowed the old wizard into the cosy room.

"Good evening, everyone," said Tonks. He was a round, fat wizard, with white hair and a white beard which was so long that he had to keep it tied up in a big knot, or he would have tripped over it.

"Good evening!" cried the pixies, and they all stood up to greet him, for the wizard was a wise old fellow and everyone respected him.

"Well!" said Tonks, taking off his long black cloak. "We have come to discuss a most important matter together – the party for the Fairy Princess this winter!"

"Won't you have a nice cup of tea and some cake before you begin the meeting?"

asked Lightfoot, coming up with a big cup of steaming hot tea. "Sit down and make yourself comfortable, Tonks."

Tonks looked round for a seat. He was fat and rather heavy, so he chose the biggest seat he could see, which, as you have guessed, was Prickles the hedgehog under his red shawl!

Tonks sat down heavily, holding his cup of tea in his right hand and a cake in his left.

But no sooner had he sat down than he shot up again in a fearful hurry, shouting,

"Oh! Oooh! Ow! Pins and needles! What is it? Oooh!"

He was so scared by sitting down on the prickly hedgehog that he upset his hot tea all over the two pixies that were next to him. His cake flew up into the air and hit Lightfoot on the head when it came down! Dear, dear, what a commotion there was, to be sure!

"What's the matter, what's the matter?" everyone cried.

"Oooh!" said the poor wizard, rubbing himself hard, for the hedgehog was very, very prickly, and all the prickles had pricked Tonks when he sat down so hard.

"Ooooh!" said the two pixies who had been scalded by the tea.

"Ooooh!" said Lightfoot, wondering what had hit him.

"How dare you put pins and needles on the seat left for me?" roared Tonks suddenly, shaking his fist in Lightfoot's face. "How dare you, I say?"

"Whatever do you mean?" said Lightfoot, most astonished. "Don't talk to me like that, please, Tonks. I don't like it. And anyway, what do you mean by throwing

your nice hot tea over my friends?"

Prickles began to think he was going to get into trouble. So he very quietly started to move towards the door. But a pixie saw him and shrieked in fright.

"Look at that sofa! It's walking! Oh, look at it! It's gone magic!"

All the pixies looked at what they thought was a sofa, walking towards the door. Tonks looked too.

"Why, that's the sofa I sat down on!" he cried. "It was as prickly as could be! Catch it! Quick! Catch it!"

Prickles was very frightened. He ran towards the door, and just as he reached it, a pixie pulled at the red shawl he had thrown over himself!

"Oh! Look! It's Prickles, the inquisitive hedgehog!" cried Lightfoot angrily. "He came here and hid himself to hear our secrets. No wonder poor Tonks thought he was sitting on pins and needles! Catch him!"

But Prickles was safely out of the door. He banged it behind him and scurried off through the ditch. He made his way through the stinging nettles, and ran to a hole in the bank that he knew very well. A big stone covered the entrance and a fern grew over the stone. He would hide there!

Tonks, Lightfoot, and all the other pixies raced after him. They did not like stinging nettles, so they went round them, and by the time they had got to the other side, Prickles was nowhere to be seen!

"Find him, find him!" raged Tonks. "I'll teach him to prick me! Yes, I will! I'll pull out all his prickles! I'll – I'll – I'll – "

Prickles heard all that Tonks was saying, and he trembled in his hole. He was safe there, and the stone and fern hid him well. He did hope that no one would find him.

No one did. The pixies hunted for a long time and then gave it up. "He must have gone to his grandmother on the hillside," said Lightfoot. "Let's go back."

"Now listen!" said Tonks fiercely. "You keep a look-out for that rascal of a hedgehog all the winter. As soon as he shows his nose, bring him to me! I'll keep a fine meal of cooked needles for him! I'll be going away to Dreamland in the springtime, so find him before then."

"Yes, Tonks," said the pixies. "We are always about this hedgerow, so we shall be sure to see him. Anyway, he will turn up for the party, so we'll catch him then!"

Prickles heard every word, and how he trembled when he heard of the cooked needles! Oh dear!

"I shan't go out of this hole until Tonks has gone to Dreamland!" he decided. "I'm not going to be caught!"

So, all that winter, Prickles hid in his little hole. He did not go out to catch beetles or slugs, but just curled himself up and slept soundly. He only awoke one night when he heard a great noise of laughing and chattering – and when he poked his nose out, he found that it was the party that was being given in honour of the Fairy Princess's birthday! Poor Prickles! He didn't dare to go to it, and he saw the toad, the frog, the squirrel, and the little brown mouse all hopping and running along to have a good time, but he had to keep close in his hole.

It really served him right, didn't it? And do you know, it's a strange thing, but ever since that winter, hedgehogs have always slept all through the cold days! Perhaps they are still afraid of Tonks! I shouldn't be surprised.

A Tale of
Sooty and Snowy

Down at the toyshop there was a big black cat, with eyes as green as cucumbers. She belonged to Mrs Kindly, who owned the toyshop, and her name was Comfy. This may seem an odd name for a cat, but it was exactly right for Mrs Kindly's cat. Comfy looked just like her name – cosy and comfortable and warm. All the children loved her.

Comfy used to sit on the counter near the teddy bears and fluffy rabbits, and the boys and girls stroked her when they came into the shop.

Two children liked her especially. They were a brother and sister, called Robert and Ruth. They always stroked Comfy to make her purr. She had a very loud purr indeed.

"It's as loud as Mummy's sewing-machine!" said Robert.

Mrs Kindly always liked to see Robert and Ruth in her shop. They were so nice to one another. They seemed to share everything. They even shared stroking the big black cat.

"Your turn to stroke her now," Ruth would say to Robert.

If ever they had any money to spend they shared it out between them, too. "Our uncle gave me a sixpenny piece," said Robert. "And he gave Ruth a box of sweets, Mrs Kindly. So Ruth shared the sweets with me, and now I'm going to share the sixpence with her. That's threepence each. Have you anything for threepence?"

"It's a pity more brothers and sisters aren't like you two," Mrs Kindly often said. "Now take John and Jane – the unkind things they say to one another! And Peter and Pam – why, I had to send them out of my shop the other day, they quarrelled so!"

Now one day Comfy the cat wasn't on the toy counter with the rabbits and the bears when Robert and Ruth came in.

"Oh! Where's Comfy?" asked Ruth.

"I'll show you," said Mrs Kindly, and she took Robert and Ruth to the little room at the back of her shop. By the fire was a cosy basket, and in it was the big black cat, Comfy. She purred loudly when she saw the two children.

"Look what she's got in her basket!" said Mrs Kindly, and the children looked. Ruth gave a squeal.

"Oh! Kittens! How many? Aren't they simply lovely!"

"She's got two," said Mrs Kindly, "and the odd thing is that one is black just like Comfy herself, and the other is white. They will make a pretty pair later on."

The kittens were very tiny. They

hadn't even got their eyes open yet. They snuggled up to their big soft mother, and she licked them lovingly.

After that, of course, Robert and Ruth came to see the kittens every single day. They watched them grow, and they were glad when they opened their blue eyes. Then the kittens began to crawl about the basket and make funny little squeaky mewing noises. The children loved them!

They told their mother about the kittens – and Comfy the cat talked about the two children in mew language to her kittens.

"They're nice children," she told the kittens. "Brother and sister, just like you are, Snowy and Sooty. And you must see that you are as kind and good to one another as Robert and Ruth are."

She didn't really need to tell the two kittens that, because they loved one another from the first day that they opened their eyes and saw each other! They played together and cuddled together, and shared the ball of wool that Mrs Kindly found for them to play with. When they were old enough to drink milk

they shared the same saucer, and they ran everywhere together.

"We should really call them Robert and Ruth!" Mrs Kindly said to the two children one day. "They are just like you two. Dear little Snowy and Sooty, I shall be sorry when I have to sell them. So will their mother-cat, she loves them so."

Comfy was upset when she heard Mrs Kindly say that. Good gracious! So her kittens would be sold – and not only that, the two would be parted from one another. One would go to one home and the other to another home. They might never see one another again!

Snowy and Sooty cuddled together and mewed into each other's furry ears. "Let's always keep together. Let's not go to different homes. Let's stay together like Robert and Ruth."

But, oh dear – Mrs Kindly soon put a notice in her window. It said: "Two beautiful kittens for sale, one white, one black."

"You'll soon be parted now," said their mother to them sadly. "Nobody ever wants two cats – so make the most of one another because you never know when someone will come in and buy one of you."

Robert and Ruth saw the notice in the shop window. They did hope nobody would buy the kittens yet – they really were so sweet now. Robert loved Sooty and Ruth loved Snowy. Each child took up a kitten and petted it.

"I shall just hate to hear that someone has bought Snowy and taken her away," said Ruth, her voice trembling. "I do so love her."

"And I shall hate to know that someone has bought Sooty," said Robert. "He's so

amusing and so quick and so cheeky! I love him, too."

Now when Robert got home that day he went to his money-box to see how much money he had. The kittens were two shillings and sixpence each. If he had five shillings he would buy them both!

But he only had half-a-crown, made up of a shilling, two sixpences, a threepenny-bit and three pennies. And by the time he could save up another two shillings

45

and sixpence, both kittens would have been sold.

He thought longingly of Sooty – black as soot, green-eyed now like his mother, playful and loving. He had enough to buy him.

But Ruth loved Snowy. If he were going to buy a kitten he would have to buy Snowy, because Ruth loved her – she would be disappointed if he bought Sooty. It was a puzzle to know what to do!

He went out to sit in the shed and think about it. When he was gone, Ruth came running into the playroom, and she took down her money-box. She had had exactly the same thought as Robert. Had she

46

enough money to buy both kittens? That would be lovely!

She counted out her money. Two shillings – a sixpence – three threepenny-bits – and a penny. How much was that? Surely it would be nearly five shillings! But it wasn't, of course. It was only three shillings and fourpence – what a shame!

Ruth put the money back. Then she too went to think about things in the woodshed. Robert had just gone. Ruth sat down and thought much the same thoughts as Robert.

"If I buy Snowy for myself – and I do so love Snowy – Robert will wish and wish it was Sooty, because he loves Sooty. But I haven't enough money for both!"

She thought again, sitting on a pile of sacks, frowning. Then she jumped up.

"Well – I love Snowy – but I love Robert more! I'll go and buy him Sooty for a very great surprise! How pleased he'll be!"

Her mother called her as she ran indoors to get her money. "Ruth! Just come and help me untangle my wool for a minute."

"Where's Robert?" asked Ruth, holding out her hands for the wool.

"He ran out in a hurry," said her mother. "He said he was going down to the village for something."

Well, I don't know whether you can guess where Robert had gone. Yes – to the toyshop! Was he going to buy Sooty because he loved him so?

No, he wasn't. He was going to buy Snowy for Ruth! What a pair! Robert wanted Sooty, but he was going to buy Snowy instead – and Ruth wanted Snowy, but she meant to buy Sooty because Robert liked him so.

Robert was in the toyshop with his money in his hand. He spoke eagerly to Mrs Kindly.

"Mrs Kindly! Has anyone bought Snowy yet? Because I want to buy her."

"Nobody's bought Snowy," said Mrs Kindly. "But dear me, Robert, I thought it was Sooty you liked."

"Yes, I do – but I'm buying Snowy for Ruth," said Robert. "Please don't say a word, Mrs Kindly – it's a surprise!"

"Well, well," said Mrs Kindly, "you're a generous fellow, Robert. We'll go and get Snowy now. Dear me – the two kittens will be sad to part. They're just as much to one another as you and Ruth are!"

Snowy was picked up and put into a basket with a lid. Mrs Kindly lent it to Robert to take Snowy home safely. Snowy mewed sadly.

"Goodbye, mother-cat, goodbye, Sooty! Oh Sooty, I do hope we see each other again! Goodbye!"

"There – she's saying goodbye to her mother," said Mrs Kindly. "And to her

brother – how those kittens will miss each other!"

Robert carried the kitten home carefully, sorry for Sooty left behind, but glad to think of how delighted Ruth would be. He went in at the back door just as Ruth ran out of the front one, her money clutched in her hand. She had finished untangling the wool and was going to buy Sooty for Robert!

She ran to the toyshop and burst in at the door. "Mrs Kindly," she said, "has anyone bought Sooty, please? I do so want to buy him."

"But I thought you liked Snowy," said Mrs Kindly.

"Oh, I do – but Robert loves Sooty, you see. I'm buying him for Robert," said Ruth. "I've only enough money for one kitten."

Mrs Kindly led the way into the room at the back of the shop. Sooty was there, alone with his mother, mewing sadly.

"Where's Snowy?" asked Ruth. "Oh – has someone bought darling little Snowy? Oh, I did so want to say goodbye to her before anyone took her! Poor little Sooty

– he's missing Snowy already. Oh dear, if *only* I'd had enough money to buy both kittens. Has Snowy gone to somebody kind, Mrs Kindly?"

"Dear me, yes – to one of the kindest persons I know," said Mrs Kindly, smiling, longing to tell Ruth who had taken Snowy. But Robert had asked her to keep his secret, so she didn't tell Ruth any more. The little girl borrowed a basket from Mrs Kindly and Sooty was put into it, mewing loudly.

"He wants Snowy," said Ruth, almost in tears. "Don't cry, Sooty. I want Snowy, too, but there wasn't enough money."

She took Sooty home carefully. She

carried him into the playroom where she could hear Robert whistling. She held the basket behind her back, her eyes shining. And there was Robert, holding something behind his back, too! It was the basket with Snowy in. He had been anxiously waiting for Ruth to come back.

"I've got a present for you – guess what it is!" said Ruth.

"And I've got one for you!" said Robert. "Guess!"

Well, they didn't have to guess, because at that very moment Sooty and Snowy

52

smelled one another's furry smell and mewed in excitement, calling to each other.

"Miaow, *miaow*!"

And when the children put the two baskets on the table, out jumped Sooty and Snowy and ran to each other at once, rolling over and over in delight!

"Why – you've bought Sooty!" cried Robert, joyfully.

"And you've bought Snowy!" said Ruth. "Oh, Robert – and I did so wonder who had got Snowy – and it was you! You'd bought her for me. Thank you, thank you, thank you!"

Mother came in to hear what all the excitement was about – and how surprised she was to see a snowy-white kitten and a sooty-black one playing together.

"What a lovely pair!" she said. "Whose are they?"

"Ours!" said Robert and Ruth together. "Oh, Mummy – we're so happy!"

So were the two kittens. They couldn't believe that they weren't to be parted after all. Robert and Ruth still have them, though they've grown into lovely big cats now. They often sit on the windowsill inside the sitting-room, side by side, and passers-by see them and stare. "What a pretty pair!" they say. "One so black and one so white. There ought to be a story about them!"

So there ought – and that's why I have written one for you!

Woof-
Woof-Woof!

"Now," said Dame Bonnet, standing up on the platform, "now we have a grand competition!"

Everyone stopped talking to listen to her. It was a very merry evening at the village hall, and the brownie band had been playing jolly tunes for everyone to dance to.

"A competition!' said Hoppy. "I like competitions. I'd like to win one some day!"

"Shh!" said everyone, because Dame Bonnet was speaking again. She held up an orange and an apple.

"It's the same competition that we have every year at this dance," she said. "Farmer Meadows is giving a crate of oranges and a crate of apples to the one who makes the nearest guess as to how many pips there are in this orange and this apple!"

Everyone cheered. Hurrah! Kind old Farmer Meadows!

"It doesn't really matter who wins it," said Dame Bonnet, smiling round. "We know that the lucky one will share the fruit with us all!"

"Not if Mr Stingy wins it!" said Hoppy to Mr Lively, who was standing near him. "So let's hope he doesn't!"

Everybody went up and whispered their guesses into Dame Bonnet's ear and she wrote down the numbers they gave her. Hoppy guessed twenty orange-pips and twelve apple-pips. Mr Lively guessed just the opposite. Old Mother Winkles wanted to squeeze the orange a little in her hand to see if she could feel the pips, but she wasn't allowed to.

"And now," said Dame Bonnet, "I am going to cut open the orange and the apple, and ask Farmer Meadows please to count the pips for me."

Dame Bonnet cut them open, and Farmer Meadows, red-faced and burly,

counted the pips very carefully indeed, one by one.

"Fifteen orange-pips and only eight apple-pips," he said. "Anyone got the answer right?"

"I did! I did!" shouted Mr Stingy, in sudden delight. "I whispered those numbers in Dame Bonnet's ear. Didn't I, Dame Bonnet?"

"Yes, you did," said Dame Bonnet. "Well done, Mr Stingy. The crates of fruit are at the back of the stage. I am sure you would like to open them now, and share your success with the others."

"Dear me, no!" said Mr Stingy at once, looking quite horrified. "They're mine. I won them fairly, and I'm taking them home for myself. They'll last me a nice long time and save me buying fruit. You can't make me open them now!"

There was a shocked silence – and then somebody hissed. Somebody else booed. Soon the hall was full of peculiar noises. Sss-sss! Boo-ooo-ooo! Sss-Boo! Boo-Ssss!

"Boo and hiss all you like," said Mr Stingy. "You'll not get a single orange or apple – no, not even a pip!"

And will you believe it, he took the two crates home right away, and never gave out a single orange or apple to anyone.

Ah, but wait, Mr Stingy! Hoppy and Mr

Lively aren't going to let you do such a mean thing, and get away with it. Oh, no! They are planning something – something that will annoy you very much tonight.

Now, about midnight that night Mr Stingy woke up suddenly. Whatever was that noise in his garden? He sat up and listened.

"Woof-woof-woof! Woof-woof-woof! Ee-oo-ee-oo-ee-oo, woof!"

"A dog! Whining and barking out there," Mr Stingy said angrily. "Waking me up like this!" He threw open his windows and shouted loudly.

"Now then! Go home, will you! Be quiet and go home!"

A loud growl came to his ears. "Urrr-rrr!" Mr Stingy was alarmed. Dear me – it sounded rather a large and fierce dog. He shut his window down a little way in case the dog jumped in.

"Woof-woof-woof!" barked the dog, and then whined dismally. "Eee-oo-eee-ooeee-ooo!"

"Go away! How can I get to sleep?" yelled Mr Stingy. But the dog wouldn't go away. It woofed and howled and whined

59

till it nearly drove Mr Stingy mad. It growled, too, so that he really was afraid of going out to chase it away.

He opened his window again and looked out. Where was the dog? He was sure it was hiding in the big bush by the front gate. He'd throw something at it and give it a fright. Then it would leap out and run away.

He looked round to see what to throw. Ah, yes – an orange! That would give the dog a fright! He had plenty in the crate. He had opened both crates and had already eaten six delicious oranges and apples.

He threw an orange into the bush. There was a yelp, and Mr Stingy grinned. Ha – that would send the brute away! But it didn't. The woofing began again, even more loudly. It almost sounded as if there were two dogs now.

Mr Stingy threw another orange. Yelp, yelp! But no dog rushed out and away. Woof-woof! *Thud* – that was another orange. *Thud-thud-thud* – off went another volley of oranges.

But that dog wouldn't budge from the

bush. It yelped and growled, but it stayed there all the time.

Then Mr Stingy went quite mad. He hurled the rest of the oranges at the bush, and as he was a very good shot he hit it every time.

"I can go out and pick them up tomorrow," he thought. "Dogs don't eat oranges. My word, there aren't any left now. I've thrown them all. All right – if that wretched dog begins to bark again, I'll start on the apples."

The dog was quiet for a minute or two, and Mr Stingy got thankfully into bed. But no sooner had he pulled the sheet up to his chin than the dog began again.

"Woof-woof-woof! Woof!"

Mr Stingy shot out of bed in a furious rage. He began on the apples. *Plonk-plonk-plonk*! Three went into the bush at top speed. "That'll teach you to disturb me!" he shouted, as loud yelps came from the bush, and out flew more apples.

At last the crate of apples was empty, and Mr Stingy yelled out of the window. "It won't be oranges or apples next, you bad dog – I'll come down and smack you!"

"Woof!" said the dog, and then was silent. Quite silent. Not a woof, not a whine, not a yelp. Mr Stingy listened for a minute or two and then crept into bed again. Would that barking begin once more? No – it didn't!

"I hope that dog has some bruises from my apples and oranges!" thought Mr Stingy. "I'll go and pick them all up tomorrow. The oranges won't be damaged, but the apples may have a few dents in them. Well, it can't be helped. Anyway, they've stopped that barking!"

The next morning, Mr Stingy went to collect his fruit – but, will you believe it, not one apple or orange was to be seen! They had completely disappeared! Mr

Stingy was amazed. He crawled in and out and under that bush for a whole hour, but not a single apple or orange did he find. He simply couldn't understand it.

Hoppy and Mr Lively came along and saw him crawling about. They nudged one another and laughed.

"What are you hunting for, Mr Stingy?" asked Hoppy, politely. "Worms?"

"No. All my fruit," said Mr Stingy, snappily. "A dog came in the night and barked until I nearly went mad. So I

63

threw my oranges and apples at him and stopped him. But now I can't find them."

"The dog must have eaten them," said Hoppy, solemnly, and Mr Lively gave a giggle. "Mr Lively, have we seen any dogs peeling oranges or eating apples this morning?"

"Not dogs," said Mr Lively, with another giggle. "Children – oh yes, children, all over the village – munching away, bless their little hearts!"

Mr Stingy crawled out from the bush at once. "What do you mean? Not my apples and oranges, surely?"

"I never even saw your fruit, Mr Stingy," said Mr Lively. "You didn't offer anyone any, you know. So how am I to know if it's your oranges and apples the children are eating?"

"I don't understand this," said Mr Stingy, furiously, and he stood upright. "I threw them at that dog, and they went under this bush! Now how could anyone know they were there, and take them for the children?"

"We're not much good at riddles," said Hoppy, grinning. "Though we might know the answer to that one, if we thought hard enough. Good morning to you, Mr Stingy. Try looking under another bush!"

They went off, laughing. Mr Stingy stared after them. Then he suddenly heard a familiar noise.

"Woof-woof-woof! Yelp-yelp! Ee-ooo! Woof!"

"Oh! Oh! It was Hoppy and Lively pretending to be dogs under my bush last night! And I threw all my fruit at them –

and they gathered it up and took it away to give to the children – which is what I ought to have done when I won the competition!" groaned Mr Stingy. "Now I haven't a single apple or orange left for myself! Wait till I get hold of Hoppy and Lively! Just wait!"

But he won't get hold of them – they are much too clever for him! I wish I'd heard them howling under that bush, don't you? What a wonderful idea.

Cowardy
Custard

Once upon a time there was a little boy called Charlie. He was eight years old, but he was small for his age. When the other boys played rough games he stood in a corner, afraid of being knocked over. They laughed at him, and pointed at him when he ran away. "Cowardy cowardy custard!" they called. "Look at him, poor little Charlie, afraid of playing games in case he falls over! Poor little cowardy custard!"

Poor Charlie! He did wish he were bigger and stronger so that he could join in the games and not fall over as soon as he was pushed. But his mother and father could not always afford to give him good meals, so the boy didn't grow as strong as he should. His father was a boatman on the river and the summer had been rainy so people had not always wanted boats. Sometimes there was not enough money to buy Charlie good meals when he needed them.

"Come on, Charlie!" cried the boys one day. "We are going picnicking. Come with us!"

Charlie went – but dear me, how he wished he hadn't when he saw that the boys wanted to climb trees to see who could go the highest! Up they went, as strong as little tigers, and Charlie stayed trembling on the ground below.

His arms were thin and weak, and he

thought he would fall if he tried to climb a tree. He was afraid that he would break his leg and then he knew his mother would be very upset.

"Come on, Charlie, climb up!" called the boys. But he wouldn't. He tried to slip away when they were not looking, but they saw him and shouted after him.

"Cowardy cowardy custard!" they called. "Cowardy Charlie, he daren't climb a tree!"

Charlie went red and ran off as quickly as he could. It was dreadful to be called a coward. If only he had been as strong as the other boys he would have been up a tree in a trice! He was sure he wasn't really a coward.

He felt very unhappy. He knew that all the other children in the school would know the next day that he had been afraid to climb a tree and he would be teased more than ever.

At bedtime Charlie lay on his back trying to go to sleep but he couldn't. It was dark outside, and the wind blew down the chimney. It was very late but still Charlie lay wide awake.

The church clock struck twelve. Charlie counted the strokes. He had heard his mother and father going to bed a long time ago. How late it was! The time went slowly on and the little boy heard the clock strike one o'clock. It sounded so loud in the middle of the night.

Then Charlie heard another sound. It seemed like a long, long howl. Charlie lay and listened. Whatever could it be? The sound came again – a long-drawn-out moan. Charlie sat up in bed. Was it a dog? He listened. The noise came again.

It must be a dog! But why was it making that dreadful noise? Where could it be?

Charlie jumped out of bed and ran downstairs. He opened the front door and looked out at the black river that flowed past the house. He couldn't see it save for a ripple here and there that shone out in the dark night. He could hear the water lapping against the edge. Then the howl came again.

"It's a dog howling in the middle of the river!" thought Charlie suddenly. "Yes, it is! It has tried to swim across and it can't. Perhaps it is drowning."

He stood there wondering what to do. He must act quickly or the dog would sink. Oh, how dark and cold the night was! Was he brave enough to find his father's boat, undo the rope and row all by himself on the dark river to find a dog he couldn't see?

Yes, he was. Without stopping to think Charlie made his way in the darkness to the mooring where his father's boat was tied up, and undid the rope. He stepped into the boat and took up the oars. He began to row over the dark water.

The dog howled again. Charlie called out to it. "All right, old boy! I'm coming! Keep up till I get to you. Where are you?"

The dog heard and gave a little howl in

reply. Charlie listened. It must be right in the middle of the river where the current was strongest. He rowed hard. The dark night was all round him, and he was quite alone – but he didn't feel afraid. He just wanted to get to the dog.

Nearer and nearer he rowed. Then he heard a splashing noise and the dog yelped. Charlie was almost there.

"I'm coming!" he called. "I'm coming!"

At last he reached the poor animal. It was so tired out that it could not climb

into the boat, but was just about to sink. Charlie took hold of it by the collar and hauled it in. It fell down in the bottom of the boat and didn't move. It was too exhausted. The little boy turned the boat round and rowed back through the darkness. He tied the boat to the post and carried the cold, wet dog indoors.

He lit a lamp and looked at it. It was a fox-terrier. It lay on the kitchen floor and didn't move. Charlie warmed some milk and poured it into a bowl. The dog lapped it up and let Charlie rub him dry with a towel. Then the boy put him gently on an old rug by the stove and left him to sleep.

Next day his father found out that the dog was a valuable fox-terrier belonging to Sir William Brown. He took it back to its owner while Charlie went to school. Poor Charlie! He forgot all about the dog when he reached school for he was so afraid of being teased because he hadn't dared to climb trees the day before.

But before playtime came, the headmaster called all the boys to him, and spoke to them.

"I have something very pleasant to say

to you today," he said. "It has come to my attention that one of my boys did a very brave deed last night, and saved the life of a valuable dog belonging to Sir William Brown. This boy heard a dog howling in the middle of the night, and got up and rowed to the middle of the river where the dog was sinking. He saved the dog and today it is safely back with its owner."

Everyone cheered and wondered who the brave boy could be. Nobody noticed that Charlie had gone as red as a beetroot.

"Now, " said the headmaster, "Sir William Brown has asked me to say that as this dog is worth a hundred pounds, he wishes to reward the brave boy who rescued it for him. He has sent me five pounds to give him in front of the whole school – and I am very pleased to know that a boy of mine deserves such a fine reward. Charlie Green, come out and collect your reward."

Charlie stood up, still blushing. All his companions stared at him with open mouths. What! Could old cowardy custard Charlie really be the boy who had done such a brave deed in the middle of a cold,

dark night? He didn't even dare to climb a tree! But he couldn't be a coward if he had done all that the headmaster had said. He must be quite a hero!

The boys began to cheer.

"Hip-hip-hurrah for Charlie! Good old Charlie! Three cheers for Charlie!" they shouted. Charlie walked up to the platform and took the envelope his headmaster gave him.

"I'm proud of you, my boy," said the headmaster, and shook him by the hand. Charlie was so pleased. He wondered what his mother would say when he reached home and gave her so much money. What a lot of things she could buy!

Nobody teased him at playtime about not climbing trees. Everybody wanted to be with him and talk to him. He was the hero of the day. He was good old Charlie who had saved a dog from drowning in the middle of the night!

And when Charlie reached home that day, eager to give his mother the money in his envelope, there was more good news for him. Sir William had asked his father to go and live on his estate and care for the two big lakes he had there. He would get good wages, a nice house to live in, and they would no longer be short of money.

"You shall have plenty of good food and milk," said his mother. "You won't be a thin little scarecrow that can't climb trees or run as fast as the others, Charlie. You'll grow into a great big boy and I shall always be proud of you."

Well, you should see Charlie now! He is bigger than any of the other boys, and as for climbing trees, why, he beats everyone else at that game! And who do you think is his best friend? The little fox-terrier he saved one night from drowning! They think the world of one another and I don't wonder at it, do you?

The Little
Clockwork Mouse

The clockwork mouse peeped out of the brick box. He liked to live there because he could get under the bricks when he wanted to hide. No one was about. The mouse crept out and ran over the floor just like a real mouse.

It peeped inside the doll's-house. It saw everything ready there for a party. Little Mrs Doll, who lived there, was giving it that night at twelve o'clock. She had invited all the tiny toys, the ones that could get easily inside the house. Teddy and the big dolls were not invited. The doll's-house was not very large, and if the big toys came to the party there was no room to play games or to dance.

So little Mrs Doll had only asked Belinda, the small girl doll; Piggy, who wasn't much bigger than himself; the yellow duck from the toy farmyard; and the two cats from the Noah's ark.

But she hadn't asked the clockwork mouse. This was a pity, the little mouse thought, for he was quite small enough to get easily into the doll's-house, and he did so like a party. He was very sad about it. He had thought Mrs Doll liked him, but now he was afraid that she didn't, and he tried to think why.

"I always say good morning to her when I meet her," he thought. "I always woffle my nose most politely at her when she smiles at me. I run errands for her when she asks me. I can't think what I have done to upset her. Well, well, it's a sad thing not to be asked to somebody's party and not know why."

The doll's-house looked very pretty, for the table was set for the party and there were small balloons hanging down from the ceiling. The floor had been polished for dancing, and shone brightly. In the kitchen there were some lemons all ready to be cut up for lemonade. The clockwork mouse could smell them. He liked lemonade.

Mrs Doll was upstairs in the bedroom dressing the two children dolls. She was talking to them as she brushed their hair.

"Everything is ready," she said, "and it looks very nice indeed. But I do wish I had some flowers to put about the rooms. That's the worst of a doll's-house – there is never any garden, so I've no flowers to pick. A house doesn't look right without flowers. But I haven't got any, so it's no use grumbling about it."

Now, when the clockwork mouse heard this, he pricked up his small ears. Flowers! He knew where there were some flowers! There were a great many daisies outside the window, growing in the grass. They were small flowers, just right for a doll's-house. He would go and pick some and put them in the vases for Mrs Doll and give her a nice surprise. He wouldn't tell her who had done it, in case she was feeling cross with him about something – he would just do it.

He ran over to the big teddy bear.

"Would you mind winding me up till you can't wind me any more?" he asked. "I want to go out into the garden, and I don't want my clockwork to run down before I get back."

Clickity-clickity-clickity-click! The teddy bear wound the mouse's key round and round and round in his side. He went on till he could wind no more. The mouse was wound up as much as he could possibly be.

"Thank you, Teddy," he said, and ran off. He went to a mouse-hole he knew, down which lived a real mouse, and made his way along the little mouse-passage and out of a hole in the wall, leading to the garden.

There were lots of daisies in the grass. The mouse chose the smallest and nibbled the stalks in two to pick them, because his paws were not made so that he could pick them properly. He could not carry them in his paws either, for he had to run on those, so he laid each daisy down as he picked it. Then, when he had enough, he picked up the little bunch in his mouth and ran back through the mouse-hole.

He crept up to the doll's-house and listened. Mrs Doll was still upstairs, getting ready. The little mouse ran in and took four vases – one from the table, one from the mantelpiece, one from the sideboard, and one from the bookcase. He went to the kitchen and turned on the tiny tap. He filled each little vase with water. Then he put them on the kitchen table and carefully placed each daisy in water with his mouth. Three daisies were enough for each vase. The daisies were very pretty, because they were pink-tipped.

The mouse carried each vase carefully into the dining-room, and set them out. How lovely they looked! Mrs Doll would be most surprised. He heard her coming downstairs, so he raced out of the house

and went back to his brick box and listened for sounds of the party.

Mrs Doll went into the dining-room to see that everything was ready, and she saw the four vases of flowers so neatly arranged – one on the mantelpiece, one on the table, one on the sideboard, and one on the bookcase. She stared in surprise and delight.

"Who has done this?" she cried. "Oh, it's just what I wanted to make the party quite perfect!"

But nobody knew who had done it. Soon the guests began to arrive. Belinda doll came first, wearing her new blue silk frock, pink sash, and tiny shoes. Then came Piggy, tripping along on his pink feet, grunting happily. Then the yellow duck from the farmyard waddled up to the party, and quacked loudly when she saw such a fine feast set ready.

Mrs Doll waited and waited for the two cats to come from the Noah's ark. But they didn't come. At last the brown bear from the Noah's ark came running up to say that the cats were very sorry, but somehow they had got shut into one of

the carriages of the toy train and nobody could open the door to get them out. So they wouldn't be able to come.

"There now!" said Mrs Doll, vexed. "We are two short. Well, Bear, you had better stay to the party. And we want one more."

"Where's the clockwork mouse?" said the Noah's ark bear, looking round. "I saw him popping in here this evening with a whole lot of daisies in his mouth, so I thought you must have asked him to the party, but I don't see him anywhere!"

"You saw him with the daisies!" cried Mrs Doll. "So that's where the flowers came from. How nice of the little creature to give me flowers when he hadn't been asked to the party! Belinda doll, go and ask him to come. He lives in the brick box."

Belinda doll ran off to the brick box and saw the clockwork mouse peeping at her. "You're to come to the party, Mouse." she said. "Hurry up!"

"But I haven't any party clothes ready," said the mouse.

"Well, here's a pink ribbon to tie round your neck," said kind Belinda doll. She undid her sash and gave it to the mouse. She tied it neatly round his neck and fluffed out the bow. "Now you look beautiful," she said.

They went to the doll's-house together. Mrs Doll gave the clockwork mouse a hug. "I'm so pleased to see you!" she said. "It was very, very kind of you to bring me these lovely flowers for my party, especially when you had been left out."

"Well, I did just wonder why you left me out," said the mouse.

"Oh, I only left you out because I thought the two cats from the Noah's ark were coming," said Mrs Doll. "And I was just a bit afraid they might chase you, as you are a mouse. I didn't want you to be frightened, you see. But now that the two cats are not coming, there is no reason why you should not come to the party too!"

"Hurrah!" cried the mouse, running round and round after his own tail. "I'm glad I was nice about it and picked you some flowers, instead of sulking and thinking horrid things. Hurrah! I do love a party!"

They did have a good time. They danced, and they played musical chairs and blindman's-buff, and they ate jellies and buns and sweets, and drank lemonade; and the clockwork mouse tied a balloon to Piggy's tail and made every one laugh till they cried, because Piggy was too round to reach round himself and undo the string!

"It's been the loveliest party!" said the clockwork mouse when he said good-night. "Thank you very much!" Then back he ran to the brick box and fell fast asleep.

The Donkey
Who Bumped His Head

Once there was a donkey who bumped his head against a tree. He bumped it so hard that he saw stars, and this surprised him very much.

"The stars fell around me!" he cried. "I saw them, I saw them! This is most important news. I must tell it to Grunts the pig."

So he trotted to the other end of the field and put his head over the wall into Grunts's sty.

"Ho, Grunts!" he said. "The stars have fallen from the sky! I saw them myself this morning!"

"This is most important news," said Grunts in astonishment. "Why, the sun might fall next! Let us go and tell Gobble the turkey."

So they went across the yard to Gobble

the turkey.

"Ho, Gobble!" they said. "The stars have fallen from the sky! What do you think of that?"

"This is most important news," said Gobble in surprise. "Why, we are none of us safe if things fall upon our head from the sky. Let us go and tell Daisy the cow."

So they went into the buttercup field, and found Daisy the cow.

"Ho, Daisy," they said. "The stars have fallen from the sky! What do you think of that?"

"This is most important news," said Daisy, nibbling a thistle in her

astonishment. "Why, it is dangerous to be out if things like this happen! I wish I could go into my shed. Let us go and tell Baa-Baa the sheep."

So they all went up the hill to where Baa-Baa the sheep was lying with her two lambs.

"Ho, Baa-Baa," they said. "The stars have fallen from the sky. What do you think of that?"

"This is most important news," said Baa-Baa in surprise. "Why, my little lambs might be hit by one of those stars, and think how frightened they would be! Let us go and tell Koo-Roo the pigeon."

So they all went into the farmyard, where Koo-Roo the pigeon was picking up corn grains.

"Ho, Koo-Roo," they said. "The stars have fallen from the sky. What do you think of that?"

"This is most important news," said Koo-Roo in surprise. "Why, I might have eaten one by mistake, and then I should be very ill. Let us go and tell Old Rover the watch-dog."

So they all went to the other end of the

yard where Old Rover the watch-dog was sitting in the sun outside his kennel.

"Ho, Old Rover," they said. "The stars have fallen from the sky. What do you think of that?"

Old Rover opened one eye and looked at all the animals.

"This is strange news," he said. "I have seen no stars falling from the sky. Where did they fall?"

"They fell this morning," said the donkey. "I had just bumped my head against the big chestnut tree in my field, and at that very moment I saw them fall. They were red and green and yellow. Oh, it was a marvellous sight, Old Rover!"

"This is a serious thing," said Old Rover, with a twinkle in his eye. "It must be put right. What will all the children do without the stars in the sky at night? They will miss them terribly."

"Do you think it was my fault?" asked the donkey, beginning to tremble. "I believe the big chestnut tree touches the sky, for it is very tall – and when I bumped my head against the hard trunk, perhaps the top branches were shaken,

and brushed the stars from the sky."

"Perhaps," said Old Rover. "What are you going to do about it?"

"I don't know," said the donkey. "Can you help me, Grunts?"

"No," said the pig. "But perhaps Gobble the turkey can."

"I can't," said the turkey. "But perhaps Daisy the cow can."

"I can't," said the cow. "But perhaps Baa-Baa the sheep can."

"I can't," said the Sheep. "But perhaps Koo-Roo the pigeon can."

"I can't," said the pigeon. "But perhaps Old Rover the watch-dog can."

"Of course I can," said Old Rover,

yawning. "Go home, everybody. I'll put the stars back in the sky tonight without fail."

So everyone trotted off home, and when night came they looked anxiously up into the sky. Sure enough all the stars were there, far too many to count.

"Old Rover is clever," said the donkey, and took him a mouthful of straw to lie upon.

"Old Rover is wise," said Grunts the pig, and took him a crust of bread to gnaw.

"Old Rover is wonderful," said Gobble the turkey, and took him a bone he had found.

"Old Rover is splendid," said Daisy the cow, and took him a bundle of hay.

"Old Rover is fine," said Baa-Baa the sheep, and took him some wool to warm him.

"Old Rover is marvellous," said Koo-Roo the pigeon, and took him a biscuit she had found.

"Old Rover is cunning!" said Old Rover to himself, as he looked at all his presents. "Now I shall be chief of the farmyard!"

And all the stars twinkled merrily just

as if they were enjoying the joke too.

His
Little Sister

James was nine and Lizzy was six. At home they often played together, but when they went to the park James wanted to play with the older children.

"I don't want to take Lizzy," he told his mother. "She's too little. She's a nuisance. I can't be bothered to look after her."

"Don't be unkind, James," said his mother. "Big brothers must always look after little sisters, just as mothers must always look after children."

"Well, I don't want to," said James, sulkily. "I'm playing with Harry and Andrew and Tim today. I don't want to take Lizzy with me – and if I do I shan't look after her, so there!"

"I am not going to listen to you when you talk like that," said Mother. "Anyone would think you didn't love Lizzy, and yet I know you do. Now don't let me hear another word – take Lizzy and go."

James went out sulkily, dragging poor Lizzy by the hand. Lizzy was sad. She did so like going with James, and it was horrid not to be wanted. "I won't play with you and the boys, James, really I won't," she said to him. "I'll keep out of your way."

"You'd better!" said James, roughly. "I'm not going to bother about you at all! Girls! They're all silly, specially when they're little like you."

As soon as he saw Harry, Andrew and Tim he let go of Lizzy's hand and ran off

with them. Lizzy went and sat down on a seat by herself. She felt very miserable. There were no little girls to play with. So she sat still and quiet, watching the boys play.

James had a lovely game of cricket. He batted, bowled and fielded, and everyone shouted that he was jolly good. When he had made fifty runs he really felt like a hero.

"You'll be playing for England one day!" said his friends, and James felt grand. The morning flew and at last it was time to go home. He looked round for Lizzy. He had seen her on that seat over there.

But she wasn't there any more. Then where was she? She wouldn't have gone home alone because she had faithfully promised her mother never to do that. She must be somewhere in the park.

James hunted all over it. He called and yelled, but Lizzy didn't come. Suppose somebody had stolen her? People did steal children sometimes. James's heart went quite cold when he thought of somebody stealing his little sister.

Perhaps she had fallen into the duck-

pond and nobody had heard her calling. He rushed to it and looked anxiously in the water. No Lizzy there, thank goodness.

Then where had she gone? He couldn't possibly go home without her. Whatever would his mother say? And Daddy would be simply furious. Lizzy, Lizzy, Lizzy, where *are* you?

It was no use looking in the park any more. Lizzy must have left it. Oh dear, there were all those roads to cross if she had tried to go home. Surely she would be knocked down if she went by herself.

Suppose she was even now lying in some hospital with a broken leg or a hurt head!

James felt his eyes fill with tears. It would be all his fault because he hadn't taken care of her. He went homewards, stopping at each of the crossings to ask the passers-by the same question.

"Please – there hasn't been an accident to a little girl just here, has there?"

He got all the way home without hearing a word of Lizzy. He was so upset

and miserable that he began to cry as soon as he saw his mother.

"Mum! Something's happened to Lizzy! She's lost – she's been stolen – or knocked down! Oh, Mum, I was so cross with her, and I didn't take care of her and now she's gone. I've come home without her,"

"Poor James," said his mother. " How dreadful you must be feeling."

"No, no – it's poor Lizzy!" cried James. "What shall I do! Oh, Mum, I'm so sorry I was unkind. I wish, I wish, I wish I could see her this very minute – I'd always take care of her, always."

Mother opened the door of the dining-room and James went in, sobbing. There, sitting at the table, eating her dinner, was Lizzy, happy and cheerful!

James rushed at her and hugged her. "Lizzy! Oh, Lizzy! I'm so glad to see you. I thought you were lost and gone for always."

"Auntie came by and saw me by myself on the seat," said Lizzy. "When she saw you were busy with the other boys she took me to buy me an ice. Why are you crying, James?"

"I'll always take care of you, Lizzy," said James, so glad to see his little sister safe and sound that he could hardly stop hugging her. "I'm your big brother, and you will always be safe with me."

"That's what the best brothers say," said their mother. And she was right. They do!

The Strange
Little Needles

Katie was sitting on the floor with Roger. They had the rag-bag between them and were pulling out all the bits and pieces. It was great fun.

"What are you looking for?" asked their mother.

"Well, I want a piece of silk to make Angeline, my doll, a new dress," said Katie, "and Roger wants a piece of blue velvet to make her a new coat. Her old coat is almost in rags."

Roger didn't see why boys shouldn't sew as well as girls.

"Here's a fine piece of silk for Angeline's dress," said Mother, picking up a piece of red silk. "And here's just the thing for her coat – a beautiful piece of blue velvet. It was a bit that was left from your last year's party-dress, Katie."

The children were pleased. Katie cut the red silk into two halves to make a dress, and then she did her best to cut out Angeline's coat.

They threaded their needles, and began. But oh, it was difficult to sew the pieces together!

Roger pricked his finger at once and made it bleed. Katie's stitches were too big, but when she tried to do little ones, the red silk slipped about.

"Oh dear!" said Katie. "Sewing is very difficult."

"I wish my finger would stop bleeding," said Roger, sucking it. "It's making such a mess of the blue velvet."

"Oh, I've pricked my thumb now!" cried poor Katie. So she had. She sat sucking her thumb and Roger sucked his finger. They looked very funny.

"Let's go out for a walk," said Katie, as the sun shone into the room. "I'm tired of sewing."

So out they went, walking in the early spring sunshine, looking for primroses in the wood. And it was whilst they were hunting for primroses that they suddenly saw the funny old woman.

She was very small – only as tall as Katie, who was eight. She had a face like a little red apple and her eyes were as blue as Angeline's. When the children saw her she was kneeling down on the ground, hunting for something in the thick grass.

"Hello!" said Katie, stopping. "What are you looking for? Can we help you?"

"Good morning," said the apple-faced woman. "Yes – do help me, please. I was taking a packet of yellow needles to Dame Sew-Sew, and I've dropped them all. It is so very difficult to find them in the grass."

"We'll soon find them for you," said Katie, and she and Roger kneeled down to pick up the strange little needles. They were all bright yellow, and were very sharp indeed. The funny thing was that they were sharp at both ends and were very difficult to pick up. The children soon pricked their fingers with them.

"If only I knew a little magic to get the needles together," said the little woman. "But I don't."

"Well," said Roger suddenly, his face going red with excitement, "I've got something magic enough to get those needles out of the grass all together without us hunting like this for them."

"Oh, what, Roger?" cried Katie, surprised. Roger put his hand into his pocket and brought out – his new magnet! You know what a magnet is, don't you? It is a strange thing, shaped like a horse-shoe, usually painted red at the top. It has strange powers, and Roger thought they were magic.

"Now," he said. "Watch the magic that my magnet can do!"

He put it down into the grass, holding it by the red middle – and at once all those little steel needles rushed to the magnet and clung to it! Yes, they really did! Not one hid itself in the grass any longer.

Roger lifted his magnet and showed the others all the needles clinging tightly to the two ends.

"There you are!" he said. "What about my magic? Isn't is wonderful?"

"It is marvellous," said the old woman, looking as if she couldn't believe it. "Simply marvellous. What powerful magic you have!"

"Count the needles and see if they are all there," said Katie. So the apple-faced woman counted each one. Yes, there were exactly fifty, the right number. She put them carefully into a bag.

"Thank you very much," she said. "I suppose you wouldn't give me that magic magnet, would you? I would so like to have it, to pick up all the needles I've lost about my house."

"Yes, you can have it," said Roger generously. He gave it to the old woman, and she was pleased as could be. "I haven't much to give you in return," she said, "but it you like I could spare one of these needles. They are all magic, you know. You have only to stick one into anything you want sewn together, and say, 'Needle, sew! Needle, sew!' and it will sew beautifully, and make anything you want."

"Oh," said Katie in delight. "That's just what we'd like. We're trying hard to make clothes for Angeline, but we do prick our fingers so."

"Well, here you are," said the old woman, and she took a small yellow needle from her bag. "Now goodbye – I must hurry. Thank you so much for your magnet."

She ran off – and Katie and Roger hurried home at top speed to try their

magic needle. Won't it be fun for them to say, "Needle, sew! Needle, sew!" and have all their toys' clothes made in a trice!

As for Roger's magic, you can try it yourself if you want to. Buy a little magnet and see it pick up all the needles on the table. You will be surprised!

The Two
Poor Children

There were once two poor children who
lived by the seaside. Their mother had so
little money to spare that she was always
glad when the summer came because then
they did not need many clothes to wear.

Their names were George and Mollie.
They loved the sands and the sea, and
every day in the summer holidays they
went to play on the shore.

They were well-behaved children, with
good manners, and the other children
liked them.

"Come and help dig a castle, George!"
shouted Billy.

But George and Mollie had no spades.
They only had two old buckets, one
without a handle, that they had found
thrown away on the beach. So they
couldn't help to dig castles.

"We're having a sailing match on the big pool today," said Jenny to Mollie the next day. "Bring your boats and we'll all sail them together."

But George and Mollie had no boats. They couldn't bathe because they had no swimsuits. They couldn't go shrimping because they had no nets. They could only paddle, or play ball with the other children when they brought out their balls.

One day George trod on some broken glass on the beach and cut his foot a little, for neither he nor Mollie had shoes for the sands. Their mother had no money to

spare for special beach shoes, and as they were not allowed to wear their ordinary shoes on the sand in case they got spoilt, the children went barefoot.

"Look at all this glass!" said George. "It's so dangerous to leave it about! Most of the other children have shoes, lucky things – but some of them like to leave them off when their mothers are not looking."

"We'd better pick up the glass then, in case they get their feet cut like yours," said Mollie. "We can use our buckets."

So every day after that the two children hunted for broken glass and put all the bits they found into their buckets. They emptied the glass into the litter-bins.

"Why do you bother to pick up that broken glass?" asked Billy one day. "You might cut your fingers."

"We are very careful not to," said George. "We're picking it up so that none of you will cut your feet. You only come down here for two or three weeks, Billy, and if you cut your feet and can't walk for some time you'll miss half your holiday! We live here, so it's not so bad

for us – but we wouldn't like to see any of you with cut feet. You are always so nice to us."

"Come and shrimp with us this afternoon," said Billy.

"We can't," said Mollie. "We haven't got nets. Look, Billy, how full of glass our buckets are today! Somebody must have been setting up bottles and throwing stones at them. That's a really wicked thing to do!"

Billy's mother saw the two poor children emptying their buckets into the litter-bin again, and she asked Billy about them.

When she heard that they always picked

up the glass so that it should not cut the children's feet on holiday, Billy's mother looked at her little boy.

"George and Mollie have no spades," she said. "They have no nets, and no swimming costumes. They only have those old broken buckets – and they use them so that you, Billy, and the other children, will not cut their feet! I think you should do something for them, as they do something for you."

"Oh, Mother! That's a good idea!" said Billy. "We all like George and Mollie, and it's a pity when they can't go swimming and shrimping and digging with us. I'll go and tell the other children, and we'll see what we can do for them."

He ran off. The other children gathered round him and heard what he had to say. They were delighted to think they could help the two children.

"Let's look in our money-boxes and see what we've got," said Lucy.

So they did. Lucy had ninepence. Billy had one and threepence. Jane had twopence. Allan had sixpence. Mary had two whole shillings. John had two halfpennies. Jenny had five pennies and a farthing.

They all brought their money to Billy's mother that afternoon. She put some of her own to it, and then took the children shopping in the town.

They bought two large wooden spades. They bought two new buckets, one red and one green. They bought two blue swimming costumes and two pairs of beach shoes. They bought a fishing-net for

115

George and a ball for Mollie. Goodness, how pleased all the children were when they got back to the beach! It is such fun to give a surprise to somebody who isn't expecting it.

"Mollie! George!" called Billy. "Come here! You are always picking up glass for us so that we shan't cut our feet. Now we want to do something for you!"

The children gave George and Mollie all the things they had bought. The two children stared at all the things in joy and wonder. They had never had so many presents in their lives!

"Oh, thank you!" they cried. "It is nice of you! Now we shall be able to do everything you do!"

They put on their little swimsuits. They took up their spades and new buckets – they were ready for anything! And now George and Mollie can dig and swim and shrimp and fish whenever the others do.

But they still do their little job of picking up the broken glass. They never forget that, whatever happens! Isn't that nice of them?

The Two Poor Children

Chirpy the Foolish Sparrow

There was once a sparrow called Chirpy who fell into a tub of whitewash. He managed to get out – but my, what a sight he was! He was white from top to toe – only his little eyes were black and they looked round him in alarm.

The sun was hot, and as Chirpy spread out his wings to dry himself, the whitewash became hard. He looked just like a little white sparrow!

"Oh, look!" a voice suddenly cried. "There's a white sparrow! What a strange thing!"

"Where?" said another voice. "Oh, yes! What a rare bird!"

Now when Chirpy heard this, he was delighted. So he was rare, was he? He fluffed out his whitened feathers and puffed out his chest. He was the only white sparrow in the world, he was sure!

He flew off to join a flock of sparrows at the other end of the garden. They looked at him in surprise.

"Hello!" said Chirpy. "I'm a very rare sparrow indeed. I shouldn't be surprised if I'm the only white one in the world. You must all find seeds for me, and bring me the best crumbs, because I am a very special kind of sparrow!"

The other sparrows listened. They had never seen a white sparrow before, and being foolish little birds they believed

all that Chirpy said. They at once tried to find seeds for him, and two of them brought him big pieces of bread in their beaks. Chirpy ate everything they brought and asked for more.

"I don't see why I shouldn't be made king," he thought. "It would be much better to have a rare white sparrow for king than a common brown one – and I never did like Twitters the King. He always ordered me about too much. It would be lovely to order him about for a change!"

So Chirpy called a meeting, and told the sparrows what he thought.

"I am white and very beautiful," he said, spreading out his whitewashed wings. "Am I not better than a common brown sparrow like Twitters?"

"No, you're not," said Twitters the King. "I was chosen because I am wise, and know all about the ways of cats and owls. It would be stupid to make a sparrow king because he was white."

"But I am very rare! I heard two humans saying so!" cried Chirpy. "You are jealous, Twitters, because you are brown. I was brown myself yesterday, but I have made myself white! You cannot do that, can you?"

"Twitters can't make himself white!" chirped all the listening sparrows. "He is not as clever as Chirpy!"

"If Twitters can make himself white before tomorrow, he shall still be king," decided an old sparrow. "If he cannot do so, we will make Chirpy king. Meet here tomorrow, everybody, and we will decide."

All the sparrows flew off except Chirpy, who preened himself on the top of the wall, anxious to show off before all the other birds in the garden. He was quite

sure Twitters couldn't make himself white, and he was most excited to think that he would be king the next day.

When the time came, all the sparrows collected together again, and there was a great noise – for they all talked at once.

"Where is Twitters the King?" said the old sparrow. "Has he made himself white?"

"No," said Twitters, coming forward. "And I wish to say that I won't be king over you any longer. You are so foolish that you don't deserve a wise king like me. Make that stupid little Chirpy king, for he will suit you well."

The sparrows were angry with Twitters when they heard what he had to say. They rushed at him to peck him, but he flew off to a near-by tree. Then Chirpy came forward spotlessly white, and the birds proclaimed him king. How proud he was! He flew up to the wall again and stood there for everyone to admire him.

But dear me, what do you think happened? It began to rain! The drops fell fast on the garden and soon all the birds were wet and flew to shelter – all

except foolish Chirpy, who sat still on the wall to be admired.

Little did he know what the rain was doing to him! It was washing all the whitewash from his feathers, and even as he stood there he turned from white to brown before all the watching sparrows! They stared in amazement and were so lost in wonder that they were almost caught by Paddy-Paws the cat, who had come stealing up behind them!

"Look out! Look out!" chirruped Twitters from his tree. "The cat, the cat, the CAT!"

At once every sparrow flew into the air and the cat just missed a very fine dinner.

They turned to look at Chirpy, who had just noticed that all his white had run down the wall. How foolish he felt! He flew away to hide his shame – but all the others flew after him!

"You're a fraud, a fraud, a fraud!" they cried. "We won't have you for king, we'll have Twitters instead!"

But Twitters wouldn't be king for a long time. Not until every sparrow had brought him a big piece of bread would he consent to be king again. And then, poor Chirpy! He was made to work hard from morning till night – and didn't he just wish he had never thought himself grand enough to be king!

The
Poppy Pixie

Grinny was a jolly little pixie. He was very clever with his fingers, and could make a hat or a cap out of almost anything. He bought rose petals from the rose-fairy, sewed them into pretty shapes with spider's thread, and then sold them to the pixies.

But one day the rose-fairy wouldn't let him have any more petals. She said she wanted them herself to make party frocks from. So Grinny had nothing to use for his hats and caps.

"Now what shall I do?" he thought. "If I don't work, I don't make money. And if I don't make money I can't buy food to eat. And if I don't have food I'll starve. So I must do something about it."

He put on his hat and went for a walk beside the big golden cornfield that rustled softly in the breeze. Suddenly the wind came down, swept off his hat, and threw it right on the top of an ear of corn! Grinny stared up at it. He couldn't get it at all. It was so far above his tiny head.

"Bother!" he said. "There goes a perfectly good hat. Now what shall I do? The sun is so hot today that I shall certainly get sunstroke if I don't wear a hat."

As he walked by a poppy that waved in the breeze, he saw below it two small green things. They were the green hat that the poppy had worn when it was still a bud.

Every poppy wears a green hat before it unfolds its red petals. Have you seen it?

126

When the poppy is ready to shake out its silky flowers the green hat splits in two and falls to the ground. It is finished with! The poppy doesn't want it any more.

It was the green poppy-hat, split in two halves, that Grinny found. He picked up the halves. They had curled up a little and were nice and stiff.

"My goodness!" said Grinny. "These are just the things for hats! With a little feather in they would be very smart indeed! Hey, Poppy! Do you want these green things?

"No," said the poppy, bending down its pretty red head. "You can have them. I have thrown them away."

Grinny picked them up and looked round for more. Beneath every poppy he found the little caps thrown away on the ground. He got as many as he could carry and then went home. How pleased he was! He fitted one on his cheeky little head, and it made a dear little long-shaped hat. He took it off and looked at it.

"If I make two holes in the side, I can fit the quill of a feather in, and the hat will look grand!" said Grinny. He looked about for something to make the holes. He found a little knife and cut the holes neatly. Then he went to where the long-tailed tit sat with her brood of tiny babies, and begged for a few feathers from her old nest. He knew that she used thousands of feathers to line it with.

She popped into the round nest and threw out about a hundred of the tiniest feathers she had collected there. Grinny was pleased.

He set to work to make the feathered hats. He made the holes in the poppy-caps, stuck the feathers in, and there were the hats, all ready to sell!

He did sell them quickly too! The pixies and the elves were always ready to buy new hats, and these really did look smart. Even the snails came to buy one each, and Grinny chuckled away to himself when he saw the snails gliding away proudly, each with a poppy-hat on its horns.

He made such a lot of money that he really felt he ought to share it with the poppies. So he went to tell them, and they listened, their pretty red heads swaying gently on their long stalks.

"We don't want any money," they said. "We don't need to buy anything. But, Grinny, we would be so glad if you would do something for us."

"Anything I can!" said the little pixie.

"Well, listen," said the poppies. "When our red petals die and fall off, we are left with our little green seed-heads. Inside are our precious seeds. Soon our green heads turn brown and hard and the seeds get ripe. They want to get out and find new homes, and sometimes they find it very difficult."

"What can I do to help, then?" asked Grinny, puzzled.

"Could you make little windows in our seed heads with your tiny knife?" asked the poppies. "Then, you see, our seeds could fly out of the windows every time the wind shakes our heads."

"What a good idea!" said Grinny, pleased. "Just tell me when you are ready and I'll come along and make the seed-windows with my little knife. I'll make them just under the piece that sticks out at the top of your seed-head, then the rain won't get in."

"Thank you!" said the poppies, and they danced in the hot summer sun.

Each day Grinny went to see if the poppies were ready for him to make seed-windows. Their red petals fell. Now only their green seed heads were left. They turned brown and hard.

"Now, Grinny!" they called to him one day. "Bring your knife and make the holes

for the windows. We are ready! Our seeds
are black and ripe."

So Grinny climbed up the green stalks
and sat on the top of the poppy-heads,
one by one. He carved out tiny windows
in the side, just under the top of the head,
with his small knife. He really did them
very well.

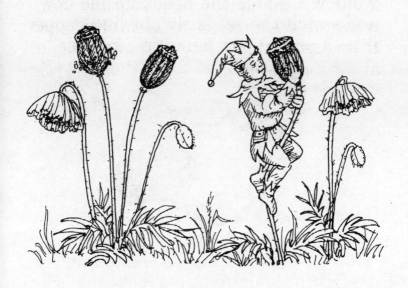

Then he slid down again. When the wind came and shook the poppy-heads, the seeds flew right out of the windows Grinny had made, and fell to the ground, ready to grow into new poppy plants the next year.

The poppies were pleased. Grinny was pleased too. The poppies gave him caps to sell – and he gave them windows for their seeds to fly from. Good!

Would you like to see Grinny's little poppy-windows? Well, find some ripe brown poppy-heads and look for the windows. Shake the heads upside down and watch the seeds fly out like pepper from a pepper-pot. Isn't it a good idea?

The
Lively Snowman

Daddy came in from the snowy garden looking angry. He stamped the snow off his boots, and called to Mother.

"Someone's forced the shed door open in the night and half my tools are gone!"

"Oh, dear!" said Mother, looking worried. "That's the second robbery. Mr Smith next door was robbed the night before. It's a pity none of us has a dog!"

"Oh, Mother – have our tools really been stolen?" cried Patrick. "Dad – are mine taken too?"

"Yes – your small spade is gone and so is the fork I bought you," said his father. "If only I knew who the thief is! I'd hand him over to the police at once."

"Were there no footprints in the snow?" asked Patrick's mother.

"No – fresh snow fell this morning,"

said her husband. "Any footprints would be covered up. Well – I must go and ring up the police."

Patrick went down to the bottom of the garden, where the tool-shed was. The lock of the door was broken. The shed looked quite empty, because so many of the tools had been taken.

"The thief came next door first – and then here – and I guess he'll go to the next house as well," thought Patrick. "That's got a tool-shed too."

The boy stood and thought hard. Suppose he came down that night and watched for the thief? He might see him and recognise him. Then he could tell the police who the man was. But how could he hide without being seen?

"I know! Of course! I'll pretend to be a snowman!" he thought, beginning to feel excited. "I'll build one today with all the other children in the field at the back of our garden. I'll build it quite near next door's tool-shed. And when the others have gone, and it's getting dark, I'll knock down the snowman we've built, and stand in his place myself!"

The more he thought about it, the better an idea it seemed! "I can borrow an old white sheet out of the cupboard and drape it round me!" he thought. "I shall look as white as snow then. There's a moon tonight. If the robber comes, he'll think I'm just a snowman – and I'll be able to see who he is. Dear me – I hope he comes!"

So that morning Patrick called his friends, and they all began to build a big snowman. It took them quite a long time. They stuck an old hat on his head, and a pipe in his mouth. They gave him a stick in his snow-hand. He really looked fine.

Patrick didn't at all like knocking him

to pieces when it began to get dark. The other children had gone home now. He was alone with the snowman. He worked hard, kicking him to bits so that he could stand in his place.

He fetched an old sheet from the house. Then he stood exactly where the snowman had been and wrapped the white sheet round him. He put the snowman's hat on his head, and took his stick in his hand. He even put the snowman's pipe in his mouth! It tasted horrid.

Then Patrick stood and waited. The moon came up. It shone down on the white snow everywhere. Patrick felt cold, and thought longingly of the bright fire in his house. He wished the thief would hurry up and come. And then he heard a little cough behind him! Someone was coming over the thick snow, across the field. Someone passed him and went to the hedge beyond.

"Hello, Snowman," said a rough voice, and the someone gave Patrick's snowman's hat a tilt as he went by. It almost fell off. It startled Patrick and made him jump.

The man disappeared through the hedge. Patrick heard him fumbling at the lock of the tool-shed there. There was a grating noise. Then a creak as the shed door was opened. The thief was inside, taking the tools!

Patrick hadn't seen who it was. He thought he would creep towards the hedge and look over. Maybe he would see the man as he came out.

The sheet caught at his legs as he tried to walk in the snow. He struggled on – and then, at that very moment, the thief came through a hole in the hedge, carrying some tools that clinked softly.

"Grrr!" said Patrick, growling like a dog, though he really didn't know why.

The thief stopped in great alarm. What? The snowman moving towards him – and growling! Then Patrick lifted up his stick as if to hit the man.

That was too much for the thief! He fled through the snow, dropping some of the tools as he went. Patrick struggled after him, wishing he hadn't wound

the sheet so tightly round his knees. He growled all the time, "Grrr! Grrr!"

The thief went across the field and over the stile. Somehow Patrick followed. The thief gave a yell as he saw the snowman still following. "It's coming after me! It'll get me!"

And then a dark figure loomed up from the shadow of the hedge and took firm hold of his arm. "What's up with you? What have you been doing in that field? Where did you get that spade and fork?"

Patrick was still struggling across the field. He saw the policeman's dark figure and yelled out, "Catch him! He's a thief! Catch him!"

So the policeman held on to the man till Patrick arrived, panting. "My," said the policeman, "you look just like a snowman. Gave me a fright, you did!"

"I pretended to be one," said Patrick, "to catch this thief! He stole my Daddy's tools last night – and he went to get the ones from next door tonight. I saw him."

"Ha! Good work!" said the policeman. "You come along with me, you wretched thief – and you come too, Snowman, and tell us your story at the police station!"

Patrick did, of course. He went to the police station, still with the sheet round him, and the snowman's old hat on his head, looking very comical indeed. The policemen laughed when they saw him.

But the thief didn't. He was taken away and locked up. And the very next day the police went to his home and found there all the tools he had stolen!

"I've got my spade and fork back!" Patrick told the other children. "And all because I was a snowman – a very lively snowman, too – you should have just seen me get across that field!"

I'd like to have seen him, wouldn't you? I would have been very surprised indeed to see such a lively snowman!

The Bad Little Scallywag

There was once a scallywag who was servant to Deep-Eyes the enchanter. Deep-Eyes kept him because he was quick on his feet and very sharp of eye – but he was a bad little scallywag, and not to be trusted an inch.

Deep-Eyes kept all his magic under lock and key, and his books of magic spells were safely in the cellar, behind a trebly-locked door.

"Oooh! You don't trust me, Master!" Scallywag would sometimes wail, when he found a drawer locked fast and couldn't open it.

"No, I don't trust you!" Deep-Eyes would say. "You are bad, and bad people are never trustworthy. If you were good I would never lock anything up, for I would know you would not pry and peep, nor steal even a pin. But, alas, you are not good!"

Deep-Eyes knew that Scallywag was friendly with greedy Dame Scuffle, and dishonest Mother Meanie. He was always afraid that Scallywag might try to steal one of his spells from him and sell it to his friends. Then they could use the spell in a bad way.

So it was no wonder he kept everything locked up, and wouldn't let Scallywag even peep into any of his magic books!

Dame Scuffle and Mother Meanie always welcomed Scallywag when he visited their cottage. They made a real fuss of him, and baked him his favourite buns. They were always hoping that one day he would be able to borrow one of the enchanter's books behind his back, and lend it to them. Then what a time they would have copying out spells and finding out all kinds of magic!

"You know, Scallywag, there's one wonderful spell in the enchanter's books that we've heard about," said Mother Meanie. "Whoever makes that spell can get all the riches and power of the world into his own hands! Think of it – you could be king of the whole world if you could only find that spell!"

"I'm not a very good reader," said Scallywag, who had been lazy at school and had never bothered to try and spell properly or write nicely. "I don't expect I could read the spell properly if I did get hold of the book."

"Well, you bring the book to us if ever you manage to get it," said Dame Scuffle. "We can read all right. Ha-ha – we could read any magic spell there is. Now, you be a clever boy, Scally, and try and get that book. It is a big blue one with yellow

edges, and it's spell number 199 we want."

"I'll do my best," promised Scallywag. "But I don't see how I'm to get the book. Deep-Eyes always locks them up so carefully."

But one day Scallywag did get his chance, because Deep-Eyes fell ill. He lay in bed, feeling very sick, and Scallywag was quite alarmed.

"I must do a magic spell to make myself better," said Deep-Eyes, at last. "Take this key, Scallywag, and open that drawer over there with it. Bring me the blue book with the yellow edges that you will find inside. And look up spell 198 for me. Read it out to me. That's the spell I must do to make myself better."

Scallywag suddenly pricked up his ears. What – that book! And spell 198 – why that was the very next spell to the one that Dame Scuffle and Mother Meanie wanted! What a bit of luck! He might be able to read it and remember it.

He scurried to the drawer and unlocked it. He brought the book to Deep-Eyes. The enchanter saw how excited his little servant looked.

"It's no use your thinking I shall leave the book lying about for you to read!" he said sharply. "All you will do is to read out spell 198 to me, and get the things to make it. Then you will lock the book away and bring me the key. I don't trust you at all, Scallywag, more's the pity!"

Scallywag opened the book, looking for spell 198. "I don't read very well, Master," he said.

"Well, try and tell me what spell 198 says," commanded his master, lying back with his eyes closed, for he had a bad headache.

Scallywag found the spell. And, oh good, number 199 was just next to it, on the very same page! He began to read out spell 198, stumbling over the words.

"For the illness of-of-of – an enchanter, take two poppy – two poppy middles, a bottle of s-s-s-sunshine, some p-p-powder from a – from a butterfly's wing – and a couple of – of smiles."

"Ah," said the enchanter. "Yes, that's right. Now, Scallywag, you know where to get all those things. Go and bring them here and mix them for me. Leave the book by me so that I can see if you have brought the right number of things."

Scallywag hurried off, leaving the book open on the table beside Deep-Eyes' bed. How he wished he had time to read the next spell! But he didn't dare to, with the enchanter's eyes on him all the time.

He found everything, even the two smiles. He collected those from two children he met and stuffed them into the bottle of sunshine. Smiles and sunshine always mixed well together, he knew that.

When he got back to Deep-Eyes, the enchanter was asleep! "What good luck!" thought Scallywag, and he tiptoed to the bed. The magic book lay open at the right page. Scallywag turned his eyes to spell 199 – the spell that would get all the

riches and power in the world for him!

He read it as quickly as he could. "Put together in a heap the following things: the roots of a high hill, two stings from bumble-bees, two stares, a mother's love, three golden hairs, a young rabbit, a blackbird's spring song, and spread over them all a mixture of sunshine and wind. Stir together, and mutter the Changing Spell. Whosoever does these things right will become the richest and most powerful person in the world."

That was the spell. Scallywag repeated it over and over under his breath, trying to learn it by heart. If only he could remember it, he would be able to make the spell himself – and then what a time he would have!

Just as Scallywag felt sure he knew the whole spell by heart, Deep-Eyes awoke. He looked sharply at Scallywag, and shut the magic book with a bang.

"Peeping?" he said. "Well, I might have guessed it. I can't trust you for a minute, can I? Have you brought the things for spell 198?"

"Yes, Master," said Scallywag, and quickly made the Get-Better Spell. It

wasn't long before Deep-Eyes was feeling quite all right again and was getting dressed as quickly as he could.

"Please can I go out to tea?" asked Scallywag, who was longing to get off and try and make the spell he had learned.

"Yes. But don't be late back," said Deep-Eyes, and strode away, looking much better. He locked up the magic book at once, of course. But it was too late – the bad little scallywag knew the spell he wanted to know!

"I don't think I'll tell Dame Scuffle and Mother Meanie!" he thought. "I'll keep it for myself. Why should I share riches and power with those two old women? I'll keep it all for myself."

So he set about getting the things for the strange and powerful spell. He soon got the stings from two bumble-bees in exchange for a pot of honey. He bribed a young rabbit to come to him, and he caught a blackbird's spring song in a rainbow net and put it into a bottle. He knew how to get the roots of a high hill quite easily, for he knew his way into the underground caves where the dwarfs lived. They gave Scallywag some roots for a piece of gold.

Scallywag said over to himself all the things in the spell – what had he forgotten? A mother's love? Well, that couldn't be bought, it would have to be stolen. So he changed himself into a baby and put himself into a pram, first hiding the baby there under a bush. When the mother came out, he stole the love in her eyes and her voice as she bent over him, thinking it was her own baby. Oh, Scallywag could be very clever when he wanted to be!

He put all he had got into a pile, and threw the rainbow net over them so that they couldn't escape. Then he rubbed his nose and thought. "There are two things I haven't got – two stairs and three golden hares. I've got the rabbit. Now, where do golden hares live?"

Well, of couse, he had read that bit all wrong! It wasn't "two stairs", it was "two stares", which is quite a different thing. And it wasn't "three golden hares", it was "three golden hairs" – the hairs of our head, not the swift-footed cousin of the

rabbit, the long-eared hare of the field!

Scallywag wasn't good at spelling. He was always making mistakes like that, because he had been lazy at school. So, quite thinking that the "stares" were stairs or steps, and the "hairs" were hares of the field, he set off to get some.

He sawed two steps off Deep-Eyes' stepladder and added them to the pile. Then he got three hares to come to him in the sunshine, which made them all golden. Now he had everything! He had only to mutter the Changing Spell over them, and spread them with sunshine and wind – and in the twinkling of an eye he would be rich and powerful!

But he couldn't remember the Changing Spell. This spell was made up of a string of magic words – and Scallywag had forgotten them.

"What a nuisance! Now I shall have to ask Dame Scuffle and Mother Meanie to help me!" he said. So off he went to the two old women, and, to their great delight and excitement, told them that he was making spell number 199!

"I've got everything for it," said Scallywag. "But I can't remember the Changing Spell. Will you come and repeat it for me while I spread everything with sunshine and wind. Then we shall all be rich and powerful."

"I shall send Deep-Eyes off to the moon," said Dame Scuffle, "and I shall take all his magic for myself."

"I shall build myself the biggest castle in the world and keep a thousand servants," said Mother Meanie. "Come along – let's go at once and say the Changing Spell. I know it by heart."

The three of them went along to where Scallywag had got all his things piled together. The old women danced round in a ring and chanted the Changing Spell.

But all that happened was that the nose of each of them suddenly grew three times as long as before! No riches or power came to them – only these dreadful noses! They stared at one another in the greatest dismay.

And just then Deep-Eyes came back. How he stared when he saw the long, long noses – and the big pile of things spread with sunshine and wind! He glanced

quickly at each of them, and saw that Scallywag had made two mistakes – there were hares, not hairs, and stairs, not stares! Ho-ho! If Scallywag had learned to spell properly at school he wouldn't have got that long nose – he would have been richer and more powerful than anyone else in the world.

Deep-Eyes took hold of Scallywag's long nose and pulled him into the kitchen. Dame Scuffle and Mother Meanie flew away in alarm. Scallywag trembled and shook.

"So you found out the spell to make

long noses," said Deep-Eyes, pretending it was a very good joke. "Well, well, well! Who would have thought that you and your friends wanted a spell for that? Well, it worked very well, didn't it?"

"Oh, Master, can you take my long nose away?" begged Scallywag, bursting into tears.

"What – you didn't want to make the spell for long noses?" said Deep-Eyes, looking closely at Scallywag. "Then what spell did you want to make? Tell me, Scally. And where did you see it?"

"Oh, nowhere, Master, nowhere!" cried Scallywag, afraid to say what spell he had really meant to make. "Don't look at me like that, Master – this was the spell we wanted to make, yes, it was – the long-nose spell. No other, Master, no other!"

"Then that's all right," said Deep-Eyes. "You've done what you wanted to do. I won't take the long noses away, because they seem to be what you wanted. And how handy that long nose of yours will be when I want to twist it, Scallywag! Ha-ha! It's a fine spell you've made, no doubt about that at all! Just the spell for greedies like Dame Scuffle, and meanies like Mother Meanie, and scallywags like you!"

Scallywag had to keep his long nose, and so did the others. But they might have known that riches and power should go to good people, and not to bad, mightn't they? They certainly got what they deserved. Scallywag's nose is longer than ever, because Deep-Eyes will keep pulling it. He says he just can't help it!

Pootoo's
Red Paint

Hickory the elf was very angry. She stood on a tub in the market-place of Cherry-Pie Village and told the people there all about it.

"I had a secret," she said, "a very nice secret. I was making a lovely shawl for my aunt, Dame Nimble, to give her on her birthday, and it was made of silver spider-thread, as fine as could be. It was going to be such a surprise for her, and now what do you think? Someone has told her! But how did anyone know? I kept it a secret, because it was to be a surprise."

"There's a peeping Tom in our village!" said Tickles the gnome. "I'm sure there is! I wrote a letter to my cousin the other day and the whole village knew what I'd written! And I didn't tell anyone!"

"Yes, and when I counted up my

157

money last week, and put it away in my money-box, thinking that nobody but myself knew how much I'd saved up for Christmas, I found that everyone knew exactly how much I had saved!" cried Jumble the brownie. "Who is the peeping Tom?"

Nobody knew. They all looked round at one another, but nobody could guess who it was.

"We shall never know!" said Peeko the pixie. "But oh, if only we could catch him! We'd spank him hard and duck him in the pond!"

"Yes, we would!" cried everyone.

"I think I know who could catch him," said Hickory. "What about Pootoo the wise man? He is coming to stay with my aunt, Dame Nimble, very soon, and he is very, very clever. He knows all kinds of spells, and he might make some magic to find out who the tell-tale is."

"Ask him," said everyone. So the next week when Pootoo arrived at Dame Nimble's, Hickory went to tea and told him everything.

"Have you any magic you could use to find out what we want to know?" she asked Pootoo.

"No," said Pootoo, smiling. "I don't need to waste my magic on things like that, Hickory. I can find that out without any trouble at all!"

"How?" asked Hickory, in surprise.

"Never you mind!" said Pootoo. "But if you will all meet in the Town Hall tomorrow morning at ten o'clock I'll tell you who your peeping Tom is! Now go away and tell everyone what I have said, and don't disturb me this evening, whatever you do, because I am going to do some very strange magic for Dame Nimble."

Off went Hickory, and told the news to everyone.

"And Pootoo says we must all meet in the Town Hall tomorrow morning at ten o'clock," she said. "Then he will tell us who the tell-tale is! Won't we punish him then! I mustn't disturb Pootoo any more tonight, because he is going to do some very strange magic for my aunt, Dame Nimble."

Now that night, as soon as it fell dark, Pootoo did a strange thing. He took a big pot of red paint and slipped out into the garden. He went round to the little kitchen window and carefully painted the wall outside, and the windowsill too, with the bright red paint. Then he ran indoors again, chuckling softly.

The next thing he did was to pull up the kitchen blind and light the lamp. Then he sat down in the chair and began to play dominoes with Dame Nimble.

In the darkness someone came creeping up. Was it an elf, a pixie, a brownie or a gnome? It was much too dark to see – but

whoever it was he had seen the light in Dame Nimble's window and had come to spy, so that next day everyone in the town might know what magic Pootoo had been making that evening.

Pootoo heard the gate creaking softly as someone opened it, for his ears were as sharp as a rabbit's, but he said nothing. He just went on playing dominoes with Dame Nimble.

Presently Pootoo heard someone leaning up against the windowsill, but still he said nothing. He didn't even turn his head to see who it was in the darkness.

The one who was peeping could not make out what Pootoo was doing. He had never seen dominoes before, and he thought they must be very strange magic indeed. He craned his neck to see everything, and nearly burst himself with holding his breath so tightly.

When Pootoo thought the peeper had peeped long enough, he yawned loudly and stretched himself.

"Dear me!" he said, looking at the window and pretending to be very much surprised. "Dear me! I've forgotten to pull down your blind, Dame Nimble. I'll do that straight away."

He jumped up, and walked slowly over to the window. The peeper slipped away quickly, and ran out of the gate. Pootoo chuckled.

"I shall know you tomorrow morning!" he said.

Now next morning everyone went to the big Town Hall, most excited to think that the peeping Tom would be pointed out at last. Hickory, Dame Nimble, Jumble, Tickles and Peeko went too, and Hickory stared in surprise at Peeko.

"Whatever have you done with your hands and your tunic?" she cried. "They're all red!"

"Yes, I know," said Peeko. "I can't think how I got them so red, because I'm quite sure I haven't been near any red paint at all. It's very strange."

"Hush now," said Dame Nimble. "Here's Pootoo."

Pootoo stood up on the platform and looked down at the people. His bright eyes searched here and there, and at last he saw Peeko.

He pointed his finger at him and everyone fell silent.

"Bring that pixie here!" cried Pootoo. Two gnomes caught hold of the surprised Peeko and took him up on to the platform, where Pootoo turned him so that he faced everyone.

"Here is your peeping Tom," he said. "Here is your tale-teller! Last night I painted the windowsill and wall outside Dame Nimble's window a bright red. Whoever came up to pry and peep would have to rub against it, and would show red stains afterwards. Well, here is a pixie with red marks on his hands and on his tunic. How did they come there, Peeko?"

"I d-d-d-don't know," said Peeko, looking terribly scared. "I m-m-must have spilt something on my tunic, Mr Pootoo."

"How did those red marks get there?" thundered Pootoo. "Were you, or were you not, peeping into Dame Nimble's cottage last night?"

Then Peeko began to cry loudly.

"Yes, I was," he sobbed. "And I saw you playing some funny magic with Dame Nimble. Please let me off and forgive me. I won't do such a thing again."

"When we were talking about it the

other day, Peeko said that the tale-teller ought to be spanked and ducked in the pond!" shouted everyone. "Didn't you, Peeko?"

Then Peeko sobbed even more bitterly, but it wasn't a bit of use. He was given one hard spank by everyone, and then Hickory and Pootoo ducked him in the pond till he was wet all over.

"I'll never, never peep and pry again!" he vowed. "Now do please let me go home and change this horrid red-splashed tunic."

"No!" cried everyone. "You must just

go on wearing it, and it will remind you of the last time that you went prying and peeping, Peeko."

Poor Peeko! He still wears his red-painted tunic, and he blushes as red as the paint when anyone asks him why he doesn't wear clean clothes! But they're falling into rags now, so I expect he will soon be allowed to get new ones. Won't he be pleased?

The Tale of
Nimble-Thimble

Nimble-Thimble was sewing-maid to the Queen of Fairyland. She could sew very beautifully indeed – almost as well as the Queen herself. She made all Her Majesty's dresses, and so small were her stitches that they could hardly be seen, even by fairy eyes.

One day she made such a lovely dress that everyone praised Nimble-Thimble, and said that surely only one person could be better than she was at sewing – and that was the Queen herself.

But secretly, to herself, Nimble-Thimble thought, "I am better than the Queen! After all, what does she do with her needle? She merely embroiders a few cushion-covers – a few tablecloths for her banquets – and not much else! Whereas I, I make beautiful gowns of daffodil petals,

hats of pimpernel red, coats of russet leaves trimmed with gossamer! The last frock I made, which was so praised, was made from cobweb dyed in the moonlight – so soft, so shining."

Nimble-Thimble sat over her work and thought these things to herself – and it was not long before she was saying them to others.

"I am the best thimble-wearer in the kingdom!" she told everyone. "I can sew better than anyone else in the world! No one can make such small stitches as I! No one can make the beautiful things that I can."

"You should not boast like that!" said an old gnome. "It is bad. And besides, you know perfectly well that the Queen, your mistress, can sew more quickly and more finely that you!"

"She can do no such thing!" cried Nimble-Thimble. "I am quite sure of that!"

It was not long before news of the little elf's boasting came to the ears of the Queen herself. She was sorry for she liked Nimble-Thimble, and found her very useful. She called the elf to her and scolded her.

But Nimble-Thimble stood there sulking and would not say a word. The Queen gazed at her in surprise, and then she spoke angrily.

"Surely, Nimble-Thimble, you do not really think you can do better than I can? Why, you are only a small sewing-maid, though it is true that you are very clever with your needle, and can make the most beautiful tucks, frills and flounces that ever I saw!"

"You sew very little," said Nimble-Thimble, sulkily. "It is no wonder that I can do things more beautifully than you can, Your Majesty."

"So you do think so!" said the Queen with a laugh. "Well, you shall try your skill with me, elf. We will each of us make a gown for dancing, and we will wear our own that we have made, and let the fairies come to judge which is the better of the two!"

Nimble-Thimble agreed and set to work eagerly. She took the purple mists that rise up in the sunset over the fields, and made a dress full of frills and tucks that swayed out like the beautiful mists themselves. And with it she made a purple cloak, on which she embroidered most beautifully the red setting sun, and below it she worked a picture of fairies sitting in the fields, clapping their hands. This was a very small picture, hardly to be seen. Indeed, Nimble-Thimble was not sure that she wanted it to be seen by anyone, for the fairies were clapping the figure of the elf herself, parading before them in a beautiful gown – and behind a tree sat the Fairy Queen, weeping because the fairies preferred Nimble-Thimble's frock to her own!

All this Nimble-Thimble put into her

tiny embroidered picture below the red setting sun on the cloak. She hoped that it would come true – and thought to herself how grand she would feel when the fairies chose her frock and not the Queen's!

The day came for the judging. All the fairies, the gnomes, the brownies and the pixies came into the big field nearby to choose between the Queen's sewing and Nimble-Thimble's. First came the elf, dressed in her marvellous misty frock. The frills swung out like creeping mist,

and the red sun embroidered on the cloak gleamed brightly.

It was a wonderful gown and all the little folk watching clapped their hands and cried out in delight. Nimble-Thimble was overjoyed.

Then came the Queen. How can anyone tell what her dress was like? She had dipped her thread in the sunshine itself, and as she walked before them her gown shone and flashed like sunbeams. It was a wonderful frock for a wonderful queen, and everyone stood up and shouted for joy to see such an astonishing sight.

"The Queen's frock is the lovelier of the two!" they cried. "But Nimble-Thimble's is very beautiful. Come here, Nimble-Thimble, and let us see it closely."

The little elf, angry and disappointed, walked before the fairies – and as she walked, the wind blew her misty cloak open, showing the setting sun embroidered on it – and the tiny picture below.

"What is this that you have sewn here?" cried a gnome – and he bent down to look closely. When he saw the boastful and

unkind picture that Nimble-Thimble had worked there, he drew back in anger.

"See what she has done!" he cried. "She does not deserve to wait upon our dear and lovely Queen! See the rude and boastful picture she has sewn!"

He ripped the cloak off Nimble-

Thimble's shoulders, and in a trice all the little folk crowded round to see what it was. They cried out angrily, and would have struck the frightened elf with their small fists if the Queen herself had not put her arms round her to protect her.

"Enough, enough!" cried the Queen. "It is my duty to punish, not yours."

The little folk went back into their ring and listened. "Send her away from Fairyland!" cried one or two.

"Yes, she must go," said the Queen, sadly. "Her gift has not been used in the right way. She must lose it, and never use a needle again."

But this was too much for poor Nimble-Thimble. She flung herself down before the Queen and cried out in despair.

"No, no! Do not take away my needle! I am only happy when I am sewing beautiful things. Send me away from Fairyland if you wish – but let me sew, wherever I must live!"

"Very well," said the Queen. "You may keep your needle – but, Nimble-Thimble, your work in future must be something that is rarely seen – for then you cannot boast of it. You must make no more dresses, no more coats, no more quilts or things that are worn or used! You shall sew all you please – but your work must be hidden. Only then will you learn to be humble, and cure yourself of your great vanity."

Poor Nimble-Thimble! She crept away from Fairyland that night, taking her precious work-basket with its tiny needles and silver thimble. She came to our world,

and here she still lives, sewing, sewing, sewing all day long.

Her work is hidden – but you may see it if you like. She can make the tiniest and most beautiful frills in the world. You will see them if you pick a toadstool and look underneath the head. Do you see those small, fine frills? They are Nimble-

Thimble's work. Look for her stitches – they are as small as ever, and only if you have eyes as good as the fairies' will you see them!

The
Bubble Airships

Once upon a time, when Jack took his bubble-blower and bowl of soapy water into the garden, he had a strange adventure. He sat down by the old oak-tree, mixed up his water, and began to blow big rainbow bubbles.

The adventure began when one of the bubbles floated upwards and disappeared inside the big hole in the middle of the old oak-tree. Jack watched it go there – and no sooner had he seen it pop inside the tree than he heard a great many excited little voices coming from the tree itself!

The little boy listened in astonishment. Who could be inside the tree? He climbed up and peeped inside – but it was too dark to see anything, and as soon as the little folk inside heard him climbing up, they became quite quiet. Not a word could he hear!

"This is a funny thing," thought Jack, in excitement. "I must get my torch and light up the hollow in the tree – then I may see something lovely!"

He ran to get his torch. He climbed up the tree once more and shone his torch into the hole – and there, at the very bottom of the old tree, deep down inside the hollow trunk, Jack saw a crowd of tiny, frightened pixies, all looking up at him with pale, scared faces!

The little boy stared in amazement. He

had never in his life seen a pixie before – and here were about twenty, all squeezed up together!

"What are you doing inside this tree?" he asked. "Do you live here?"

The pixies chattered together in high, twittering voices. "Shall we tell him, shall we tell him?" they cried. Then one of the pixies looked up at Jack and said, "Little boy, you have a kind face. We will tell you why we are here. The green goblins caught us yesterday and cut off our wings. They wanted us to tell them all the magic spells we knew, and because we wouldn't they shut us up in this hollow tree."

"But why can't you get out?" asked Jack.

"Well, our wings are gone," said the pixie sorrowfully, "so we can't fly – and the tree is much too difficult to climb inside – so here we are, prisoners – and the goblins will come again tonight to try and make us tell them what we know."

"I'm sorry about your wings," said Jack. "Won't you ever be able to fly again?"

"Oh yes," said another pixie. "They will grow again – but not for four weeks."

"What were you so excited about just now?" asked Jack. "I was blowing bubbles when I suddenly heard you chattering away in here, and that's what made me come and look."

"Well, one of your bubbles suddenly blew down into the tree," said a pixie. "And it gave us such a surprise. We grabbed at it – but it broke and made us all wet!"

"I wish I could get you out," said Jack.

"But I can't possibly reach down to you – the tree is so big, and you are right down at the bottom."

"No, I'm afraid we shall have to stay locked up here," said the pixies sadly.

But suddenly one of the pixies gave a shout and cried, "I know! Could the little boy blow some bubbles down into the tree for us? Because if he could, we might make some buckets of grass and fix them to the bubbles – get into the baskets and float off!"

"Good idea!" shouted everyone. "Little boy, will you do it?"

"Yes, rather!" cried Jack. "I'll go and pick you some grass first. Then you can be weaving little baskets of it while I fetch my soapy water and my bubble-blower. I shall have to be careful not to spill the water when I climb up the tree!"

In a short while Jack had picked some grass and dropped it down to the pixies. They at once began to weave strong little baskets with their tiny fingers – baskets quite big and strong enough to carry them away! Jack climbed down again and picked up his water and bubble-blower. Very

carefully he climbed up the tree once more, holding his bowl of water in one hand, and pulling himself up the tree with the other.

He carried his bubble-blower in his mouth, so that was quite safe. He switched on his torch and looked down into the tree again. The pixies had made some beautiful baskets, with long blades of grass sticking up from them for ropes.

"You will be able to make lovely airships with those baskets hung beneath my bubbles," cried the little boy. He blew a big blue-and-green bubble and puffed it into the tree. A small pixie held up his green basket to it as it floated down. The grass caught on to the soapy bubble and the basket swung there, just like the underneath of an airship! The pixie climbed into it, and the others gave him a gentle push. Off he floated up the tree,

and as soon as he came out into the sunshine, Jack blew the bubble away from the leaves and branches so that it would not burst. It floated gently to the ground and burst there with a little pop!

The pixie tumbled out of the basket on to the ground, laughing in delight to think he had escaped from the tree.

Jack blew some more big bubbles, and they floated down the hole in the tree. Some of them burst before they reached the pixies, for they bumped against the sides of the tree, but those that reached the bottom had the grass buckets fixed to them in a trice – and then up came the pixies, each in his own little bubble airship!

Jack laughed to see them. They really did look funny, floating along in their tiny airships. The last pixie of all had no one to push him out of the hollow tree and he broke two or three bubbles trying to push himself off; but at last he managed to float upwards too, and soon he was on the grass with the others, laughing and talking in excitement.

"We shall run away to a rabbit-hole we

know and hide there till our wings have grown," said a pixie to Jack. "It's so kind of you to have helped us. Goodbye! We may see you again some day! Won't those goblins be angry tonight when they find we have gone!"

They all ran off and left Jack alone with his bubble-blower. How excited he was to think of his strange adventure with it!

Who would have thought that he could blow bubble airships?

The pixies rewarded Jack for his kindness. They found out where his little garden was, and they kept it well-weeded and well-watered for him, and made his flowers the biggest and loveliest in the garden. I know, because I have seen them!

Timothy's
Egg

Timothy found the egg just as the sun was setting. It was a very peculiar one, for it was bright blue at one end, bright green at the other, and in the middle was a wiggly red line.

"Now this is strange!" said Timothy, picking it up. "I've never seen an egg like this before, no, not in all my ten years!"

He looked at it carefully, and he put it to his ear, and listened. He could hear a tiny squeaking going on inside the egg!

"It must be ready to hatch!" said Timothy. He put it on the grass and watched. Soon the shell broke at one end, and a sharp beak stuck out. It broke the shell all round the middle of the egg, and then the tiny bird inside popped out its head.

It was very strange-looking! It had a

bright green beak, a bright blue body, and a bright red patch on the back of its head! It wriggled out of the shell and chirped like a grasshopper.

"Well, if you aren't the funniest-looking bird I ever saw!" said Timothy in astonishment. "I wonder what you are."

"I'm a dimity bird!" squeaked the little creature, much to Tim's amazement. "Watch me grow!"

Timmy sat down on a low branch and watched the bird. It was a very surprising creature. It grew almost as quickly as a

balloon grows when you blow it up! Soon it was nearly as big as Timmy, and hopped up on the branch beside him.

"I'm a dimity bird, I'm a dimity bird!" it sang, in a low, husky voice. "I bring good luck, for I'm a dimity bird!"

"What sort of good luck do you bring?" asked Timothy, in excitement.

"Wait and see!" said the dimity bird. "Watch me grow!"

It grew some more. It grew until it was twice as big as Timmy, and then three times as big! Then it flapped its funny wings, and sang again.

"Wait a minute," said Timothy. "Just tell me this. How can I get the good luck you bring?"

"Pick up the bits of my broken shell and carry them in your pocket till you meet a person called Kate Troodlum," said the dimity bird. "Then good luck will come to you at once, as soon as ever you've met her! Oho! I'm a dimity bird, I am."

With that it spread its wings and grew about four times larger while it flapped them! Then, when it was as big as a small aeroplane, it flew right away into the sky,

growing smaller and smaller until it was a tiny speck – and then it disappeared altogether.

"This is the funniest thing that ever happened to me!" said Timothy. He got down from the branch, and carefully collected the bits of broken shell. He put them into a matchbox, and stuffed it into his pocket. Then he walked off whistling.

"As soon as ever I meet Kate Troodlum, I shall find my good luck!" he thought. "I'd better go travelling and find her."

So he started out. That was years and

years ago, and he hasn't found anyone with that name yet. If yours happens to be Kate Troodlum, do let Timmy know. He's so tired of waiting for his good luck to come to him!